Carter Grayson

New York Times, USA Today & Wall Street Journal
Bestselling Author

Sandi Lynn

Carter Grayson
Copyright © 2018 Sandi Lynn Romance, LLC

Photo & Cover Design by: Sara Eirew @ Sara Eirew Photography

Editing by B.Z. Hercules

Table of Contents

Prologue

The memories of that day would stay with me forever. Even twenty years later, it still felt like it happened yesterday. The vivid pictures in my head were like a movie reel that wouldn't stop playing, but despite the tragic events that took place that day, I lived my life in peace.

I could hear the scrambling of people, fire trucks, and sirens. The voices of the men and their footsteps as they walked through the horrific scene that was in front of them echoed in the distance.

"My god, I can't believe this," one man spoke in a horrified voice.

I opened my eyes and began to slowly crawl out from the debris and ruble that engulfed me. As I stood up, a man who stood tall stared at me from a distance, his face impaled with shock.

"There's a survivor! A child!" he shouted as he made his way over to me.

The pink dress with the white daisies my mom had bought me was torn and stained with black. One of my white patent leather shoes was missing and blood poured down my leg as I looked at the open wound. When the man reached me, he bent down and grasped my shoulders, staring at me with teary eyes.

"You're going to be okay, sweetheart," he spoke as he hugged me.

He picked me up and I wrapped my legs around his waist and my arms around his neck. As he carried me from the site, I gently smiled as I stared at the shadowy figures that were making their way back home. They were at peace and filled with light. I wanted to follow them, but it wasn't my time, and at the tender age of five, I fully understood what that meant.

I remember the sun hitting my face as he carried me out from the debris and laid me down on the stretcher that was waiting for me. People hovered with shocked expressions on their faces as they took my vitals and scrambled around while tears fell from their eyes in disbelief that I was alive. I was transported to the hospital, where I was treated by a tall and handsome young doctor who made me feel safe.

"What's your name, sweetheart?" he asked as he examined me.

"Zoey."

"Nice to meet you, Zoey." He gave me a friendly and warm smile. "I'm Dr. John Benson. Do you know your last name?"

"Anderson."

"You're safe here and we're going to take good care of you. I don't want you to be afraid."

"I'm not afraid," I spoke in a soft voice as I reached for his hand. In that moment, on that day, my life was forever changed.

Chapter One

Twenty Years Later

Zoey

I raced down the stairs and grabbed my purse from the table. I was almost out the door when I heard my dad yell my name.

"Zoey, stop!"

"Yeah, Dad?" I smiled as I turned and looked at him.

He tapped his cheek with his finger.

"Sorry." I ran over to where he was standing and gave him a kiss.

"Be careful and tell Holly I said hi."

"Always am, and I will."

I flew out the door, running late as usual, to pick up my best friend Holly for a day trip to New York City. As I climbed into my Jeep Grand Cherokee, my other dad pulled up.

"Where are you off to?" he asked with a smile.

"I'm picking up Holly and we're going to do some shopping in the city."

"Ah. Tell her I said hi and be careful."

I rolled my eyes with a smile. "Always am, and I will."

"Love you, Zoey."

"Love you too, Dad. I'll see you tonight."

I pulled up to Holly's house where she stood in the driveway, looking at her watch.

"It's about time, Zoe," she spoke as she climbed into the car and shut the door.

"Sorry. I was on the phone talking to Brendan as I was getting ready."

"What's going on with you two anyway?" she asked as she chomped on her gum. "I thought you were on a break?"

"We are, but he thinks he wants to get back together." I rolled my eyes.

"He thinks? He actually said that? What did you say?"

"I told him that he needs his space, and if it was meant to be, then it would be in due time."

"Good answer." She grinned. "You aren't really into him that much anyway. Are you?"

I shrugged. "I wanted to be, but I just don't feel that connection."

"Well, all I can say is if you aren't feeling it after eight months, it's never going to be there."

Holly Stanfield had been my best friend since my parents moved to Greenwich, Connecticut when I was five years old. She was the only person who knew my real story. We were soul sisters who told each other everything. We were inseparable. Her parents knew a different version of my life. The version of John and Scott, my fathers, who adopted me when I was a baby after I was found on the stairs of the church they attended. That was the story we had stuck with since I was five years old because if the media found out who I really was, the chaos would start all over again. I trusted her. She never told a soul and I knew she never would. She was a beautiful girl who stood five foot five, slender build, long wavy auburn hair and eyes that looked like emeralds.

While she attended beauty school, I was at the University of Connecticut getting my bachelor's degree in nursing with a specialty in hospice care. Since it was a two-hour drive from where I lived, I stayed on campus during the week and came home every weekend. I completed my bachelor's degree in less than four years, taking on several extra classes during the summer months. The one thing I loved about my job was the traveling aspect of it. I didn't work out of a facility or hospital. My patients who required hospice care preferred to do it in the privacy of their home. Most of the time, I lived with them when their life expectancy was as little as two weeks, with the exception of Charles, a fifty-year-old man who was dying from lung cancer and lived four weeks longer than the doctors expected. The way people found me was on a site called HospiceCareforYou.com. I had a profile, background check, and my list of experiences. Since I was only twenty-five, some thought I was way too young with not enough experience to care for their loved ones, until they met me.

"So now that Mr. Patterson passed away, what's your next job?" Holly asked as we walked down Fifth Avenue and did some window shopping.

"I don't have one yet, but I'm not worried. Someone will message me soon." I smiled.

"With the money you make from those families, you can afford not to take care of a few patients for a while."

"True, but you know I don't like to go too long without working. There are patients out there that need me."

"I don't know how you do it, Zoey." She hooked her arm around me. "I need coffee."

"Me too." I smiled. "There's a Starbucks right around the corner."

As we entered through the doors to one of my favorite coffee shops, we were both surprised there wasn't a line.

"May I help you?" the blonde barista asked as we walked up to the counter.

"Two Grande Americanos, please."

"I'll go get us a table," Holly spoke.

"Anything else?" the barista asked.

My eyes diverted over to where the muffins sat behind the glass.

"One chocolate chip muffin." I grinned.

"Coming right up."

I grabbed my muffin from the counter and patiently waited for our Americanos to be made.

"Two Grande Americanos for Zoey." The cute guy with the short brown hair behind the counter smiled.

"Thank you." I smiled back.

I grabbed the coffees and took them over to the table where Holly sat. Pulling the muffin from the bag, I set it in the middle of the table for the two of us to share. We sipped our coffee, picked at the muffin, and we laughed at a funny video our friend Morris sent Holly.

"Could the two of you take your laughter outside? I'm on a phone call," an incredibly attractive but rude man sitting at the table next to us spoke.

We both stared at him in disbelief that he had the nerve to tell us that in a public place. Actually, it was Holly giving him the dirty look. My eyes were fixated on how handsome he was.

"Dude, this is a public place. Maybe you should take your phone call outside," Holly snapped at him.

He looked at me with his sapphire blue eyes and I gulped at his cold gaze. He hung up the phone, got up from his seat, and stood in front of our table.

"This may be a public place, but it's not a child's playground," he spoke in an authoritative tone.

I couldn't help but admire his almost perfectly symmetrical face with a hint of scruff that graced his jawline. He turned around and I watched him walk away and out of the coffee shop. He stood approximately six foot two with brown hair that was in a classic taper cut with the top just long enough to run a comb through. His build looked hard and lean and the black designer suit he wore was tailored to perfection. He was almost perfect, except for the darkness that resided inside him, something I picked up on the moment he spoke to us.

"What a dick!" Holly laughed.

My eyes never left the doorway of the shop as Holly snapped her fingers at me to quickly bring me back to reality.

"Zoey, what the hell?"

"What?" I looked at her.

"Oh my God, don't tell me you thought he was hot." She laughed.

I picked up my coffee cup and took a sip from it.

"He was cute. You can't deny that," I spoke.

"Doesn't matter. He was rude and the type of person who thinks they own the world. I can't stand people like him."

Chapter Two

Carter

Shaking my head, I walked out of Starbucks and headed back to the office. "Immature idiots," I mumbled to myself. I arrived at the office and told Breanna, my secretary, that I didn't want to be disturbed. Today was already a shit show and I was going to explode if anyone else pissed me off.

"No phone calls and no disturbances, Breanna," I scowled as I walked past her desk.

"Sure, Mr. Grayson."

Slamming my office door, I took a seat behind my desk and brought up the projections on my computer for the shopping center I wanted to acquire. As I was in deep concentration going over numbers, my cell phone rang. It was Nora.

"Nora, I can't talk right now."

"I just wanted to let you know I fired that ratchet bitch of a nurse you hired," she tiredly spoke.

"For fuck sake. Why?"

"Because I didn't like her attitude. So, you're going to have to find someone else."

I sighed into the phone.

"She's the third nurse in a month you fired. You can't keep doing this!"

"Then find me someone with a personality and I won't have to."

"Is Sadie still there?" I asked.

"Yes. She said she'd stay until you got home," she replied.

"Fine. I'll call the agency right now and set up some interviews. I have to go. I'm very busy."

"Carter, wait. I want to interview them with you. Conduct the interviews at the house. I need to get a feel for these people before you hire them. This is the end of my life and I refuse to spend it with an uncaring monster nurse!"

I took in a deep breath to calm myself.

"Fine. Now I have to go. I'll see you later."

As I threw my phone across my desk, my friend and vice president, Ross, walked in.

"Someone sure as hell pissed you off." He smiled as he took a seat across from me.

"Now is not a good time, Ross."

"Breanna warned me you were in a mood and didn't want to be disturbed, but this can't wait." He threw a file across my desk. "Cecil Campbell upped the price of the Long Island property."

I opened the file and looked at it.

"That son of a bitch. We've been working on this deal for the past six months. The property isn't even worth this much. What the hell is he thinking?"

"I can guarantee that his gambling debt increased," Ross spoke.

"Get Lucas on it right away and stall Cecil. Tell him I'm thinking about it and I'll have an answer for him next week."

"Okay. What was that phone call about?"

I sighed as I leaned back in my chair.

"Nora fired another nurse."

"Again?" Ross cocked his head.

"Yep. As much as I love my sister, she's really pissing me the fuck off. I don't have time to deal with this shit."

"I might be able to help you out," he spoke.

"How?"

"My cousin, Reggie, hired a hospice nurse for his father-in-law who lived with him and Samantha, and he just recently passed away. From what Reggie said, this nurse was a godsend. She was amazing and took very good care of him right up until the end. And if you knew his father-in-law, he was a bastard. I can call him and get her number if you want. It might save you some trouble."

"I guess. What does it hurt? Nora wants to be in on the interview since I seem to make piss poor choices in hiring nurses for her."

He gave me a small smile before walking out of my office.

"I'll go call him now."

"Thanks, Ross."

"No problem, man."

About thirty minutes later, as I was leaving the office, Ross stopped me in the hallway.

"You leaving already?" he asked.

"Yeah. I need to get home to Nora."

"I have that number for you. Reggie said you won't be disappointed." He handed me a white piece of paper.

I unfolded it and stared at the women's name and number.

"Thanks, Ross. I'll give her a call."

"You're welcome. I hope it works out." He patted me on the back.

I climbed into the back of the Bentley and told Juan to take me home. Pulling out my phone, I dialed the number on the piece of paper.

"Hello," a soft voice answered.

"Hello. Is this Zoey Benson?"

"Yes. Who's this?" she asked.

"My name is Carter Grayson and I received your number from a friend of mine. I understand you're a hospice nurse?"

"Yes, I am."

"I'm hoping you're available for an interview. My sister is in need of a hospice care nurse and you were highly recommended."

"When would you like to schedule the interview?" she asked.

"As soon as possible. Actually, if you're available, let's say about an hour."

"It depends, Mr. Grayson, what's your address?"

"212 Fifth Avenue, Apt. 21A."

"That's perfect. I'm already in the city, so I can meet you in an hour."

Her words caught me off guard. *Didn't she live in New York?*

"I'll see you then." I ended the call.

She sounded young. Too young, in fact. Maybe she was just one of those women who sounded differently on the phone. As soon as Juan dropped me off in front of my building, I climbed out and was greeted at the door by Joseph, the doorman.

"Good afternoon, Mr. Grayson." He nodded as he held the door open for me.

"Hello, Joseph. I'm expecting a woman by the name of Zoey Benson for an interview in about an hour. Just send her up."

"Ah, I did see the last nurse leave here with her suitcase a few hours ago. Another one bites the dust, eh?"

I heavily sighed. "It seems no one can make Nora happy these days."

I headed to the elevator and took it up to my penthouse. When the doors opened, I stepped out, set my briefcase down, and headed to the kitchen where Sadie was cooking dinner.

"Where is she?" I asked.

"In her room lying down."

I headed out of the kitchen and down the hallway to Nora's room. The door was slightly opened, and when I peeked inside, I saw she was awake.

"Are you okay?" I asked as I stepped inside.

"I'm really tired." She turned her head and looked at me.

"I have someone coming here in a little under an hour for an interview. She came highly recommended by Ross's cousin. Do you feel up to it?"

She gave me a small smile as her eyes slowly closed.

"I'm up to it. Just wake me when she gets here."

"Okay. Get some rest."

I walked out of her room with a sick feeling in the pit of my stomach. Watching her condition deteriorate was slowly killing me inside. I was already dead and didn't think that anything else could happen to make me feel the way I felt. The numbness inside me intensified as I was already a lifelong prisoner inside my own body.

I heard the elevator ding, so I headed to the foyer just as the doors opened and stood there in shock, as did the woman standing in the elevator.

"You have got to be kidding me," I spoke with an irritated tone.

"You're the man from Starbucks," she spoke as her eye narrowed at me.

She stepped off the elevator and stood in front of me.

"Zoey Benson." She extended her long, elegant hand.

"Carter Grayson," I replied as I looked at her hand and dismissed it.

She looked at me and lowered her hand to her side.

"How old are you?" I asked.

"Twenty-five." Her brow arched.

"You're definitely too young, and at that age, I don't feel you have enough experience."

"Okay, then. Am I to assume this interview is over?" she asked.

"Carter?" I heard Nora's voice coming from down the hall. "Is she here?"

Zoey shot me a look, and with a small smile splayed across her face, she pushed past me and walked over to where Nora was sitting in her wheelchair.

Chapter Three

Zoey

"Hi, I'm Zoey Benson." I reached down with a smile and placed my hand on hers.

"It's nice to meet you, Zoey. I'm Nora Grayson. Would you mind if we conducted this interview in my bedroom? I need to lie down."

"No, of course not. Let me help you," I spoke as I wheeled her into her room.

After helping her out of her chair, I tucked her in and took a seat in the white leather chair that sat next to her bed. Carter Grayson stood in the doorway and watched my every move with a pissed off look on his face. It was the same look he had at Starbuck's earlier in the day when he walked over to me and Holly.

"Carter, get in here," Nora spoke. "Don't be rude."

He stepped inside the room and took a seat on the edge of Nora's bed. I couldn't believe that he was the man from Starbucks. He stared at me and I stared back. His eyes burned through mine as I stared at the aura of darkness that surrounded him.

"I have stage four brain cancer," Nora spoke. "And my time is coming to an end, so I need someone who is available to live here full-time and work with me."

I reached over and lightly took hold of her hand.

"I'm sorry."

"Thank you, but I've made peace with everything. I guess when your time is up, it's up. Right?" She gently smiled.

"Nora, that's enough!" Carter snapped. "How much experience could someone your age really have, Miss Benson?"

"I can assure you, Mr. Grayson, that I have more than enough experience in hospice care."

"What? Two years' worth?"

"Three. I can give you references if you don't believe me," I spoke.

Nora stared at us and didn't say a word. It was strange to me that she just lay there, almost as if she was trying to read the both of us.

"It doesn't matter to me. I'd like to hire you, Zoey," she spoke. "Carter will go over all the details with you and then you can make your decision whether or not you're interested in taking the job. But I hope you do." She smiled. "Carter, I need to rest now. Take Zoey out and the two of you can talk."

"Nora."

"Carter, please."

He took in a sharp breath as he got up from the bed and asked me to step out into the hallway.

"We'll talk in my office," he spoke rudely as I followed him. "Have a seat."

"How long does she have?" I asked as I took a seat across from his desk.

"About two months. The tumor had progressed so rapidly that there was nothing the doctors could do. This isn't her first battle with cancer either. When she was sixteen, she was diagnosed with non-Hodgkin's lymphoma. She underwent a round of chemo and went into remission. If you accept the job, you will be paid on a weekly basis. You will be required to move in and you will be responsible for her care 24/7. Still interested?" His brow arched.

"Yes." I smiled. "I am very interested."

"I'm not going to lie to you, Miss Benson. I'm not happy about this, and if it were up to me, I wouldn't hire you. Your lack of experience concerns me. But Nora has fired the last three nurses I've hired and she really seems to like you, so you can thank her. I'll need you to start tomorrow. Will that be a problem?"

"I can start tonight," I spoke. "I'll just have to go home and pack some things. I can be back here later."

"Where is home for you?" he asked as he narrowed his eye. "You mentioned over the phone you were in the city."

"Greenwich, Connecticut."

"I see. Tomorrow morning will be fine. You won't need your car because Nora has her own driver on standby. You can pack your things tonight and I will send my driver, Juan, to pick you up around nine a.m. And by the way, your maturity level needs some heightening. I will not tolerate that kind of behavior you displayed in Starbuck's in my home and around my sister. Do you understand?"

I sat there in shock at the way he spoke to me. Who the hell did he think he was? Unfortunately, he was going to be my boss and I had no choice but to put up with his mean and disrespectful attitude towards me. Plus, Nora needed me and I wasn't going to let her down in her final stage of life. I would make sure she had the best possible care I could give her.

"Why are you staring at me like that?" he asked.

"It's nothing. Are we finished here?" I asked as I stood up from my chair.

"Yes."

I walked to the door and placed my hand on the knob. As I started to open it, I turned and looked at him.

"Laughter is good for the soul, Mr. Grayson. You should try it some time."

I walked out of his office and peeked in on Nora before leaving.

"Hi." She smiled as I stepped inside. "I hope my brother wasn't too much of an asshole."

"He was, but I've accepted the job anyway and I will be back in the morning. Is there anything I can do for you before I leave?" I placed my hand on her arm.

"I'm fine. Thank you. Thank you for taking the job."

"You're welcome. Get some rest and I'll see you tomorrow."

I pushed the elevator button and waited for the doors to open.

"I thought you already left," Carter spoke.

"I wanted to make sure Nora didn't need anything."

"Your job starts tomorrow, Miss Benson," he growled.

"Don't worry about it, Mr. Grayson. I won't charge you for checking in on your sister tonight."

The doors opened and I stepped inside and pushed the button to the lobby. As I stood there, Carter Grayson stood on the other side, staring at me with his hands tucked into his pants pockets as the doors slowly closed.

****

Carter

Fuck if she wasn't beautiful. I noticed it in Starbucks and I noticed it even more tonight. She stood five feet six inches tall with a lean body that you could tell she took very good care of. Her wavy blonde hair fell over her shoulders and her bright blue eyes reminded me of the ocean on a crystal clear day. They were full of light, like the way the sun reflects off the water. Her lips were perfectly shaped and the corners of her mouth had a slight curve, giving off the illusion that she was always smiling, even when she wasn't. She had an attitude and I didn't think she knew exactly to whom she was speaking. I'd give her one chance, and if she fucked up, she'd be out.

I went to check on Nora, and as soon as I lightly pushed open the door, her eyes opened.

"I'm sorry. I didn't mean to wake you. Do you need anything?"

"No. I'm fine. I like her, Carter."

"Who?"

"Zoey. There's something about her that makes me feel not so afraid. I felt it the moment I met her."

"You just like her because she's young."

"No. You're wrong. I can't explain it. Did you feel it too?"

"No. I didn't, and to be honest, I don't like her. I think she has an attitude and a smart mouth, not to mention her extreme lack of experience."

She let out a light laugh.

"Good, we need someone like that around here, and as for her experience, she has enough as far as I'm concerned."

I sat on the edge of the bed and glared at her.

"Oh come on, Carter."

"She's all yours, Nora, but don't expect me to be nice or go out of my way to accommodate her."

"Would it kill you for once to be nice?"

"Tell me where being nice has gotten me?" I got up from the bed and walked towards the door. "If you need anything, let me know. I'll be in my office."

Chapter Four

Zoey

I climbed into my car where Holly was sitting in the passenger's seat with her earphones in.

"Hey, how did it go?"

"I got the job." I smiled. "But you're never going to believe who I'm working for."

"Who?" she asked with a perplexed look on her face.

"You're just not going to believe it." I shook my head as I pulled out of the parking space and headed home.

"Zoe, come on. Spit it out."

"Remember the man from Starbucks earlier today? The rude but sexy one?"

"Yeah." She extended the word slowly.

"It's him. Well, I'm taking care of his sister."

"Shut the fuck up? You are not!" she exclaimed.

I couldn't help but laugh.

"Yes, Holly, I am. His name is Carter Grayson and his sister is Nora."

Immediately, her fingers began viciously typing on her phone.

"Shit," she spoke.

"What?" I glanced over at her.

"He's like a thirty-year-old billionaire. He's the CEO of Carter Enterprises and this article calls him a real estate genius and mogul. So, I guess this guy could pretty much own the world." She laughed.

"Guess so. But even though he has everything he could possibly want, there's something going on with him."

"You know what they say: Money can't buy happiness." She smirked.

"He's just so dark. To be honest, I've never experienced anyone like this before."

"It doesn't matter, Zoe. You're hired to take care of his sister, not him."

"I know." I sighed.

I dropped Holly off at home, and when I walked through the door of my house, both my dads were sitting on the couch.

"Hey, sweetie." John smiled. "How was your day?"

I walked over and gave them each a kiss on their cheek.

"It was eventful. That's for sure."

"What happened?" Scott asked.

"I got a job in the city taking care of a terminally ill patient with brain cancer."

John arched his brow.

"Well, that's good, but how? You didn't say anything about an interview."

"Mr. Grayson just called me today. He said he got my number from the family member of one of my previous patients. It just so happened I was already in the city, so we met. I start tomorrow. He's sending his driver to pick me up at nine o'clock."

"His driver?" Scott asked. "Who is this guy?"

"His name is Carter Grayson."

"*The* Carter Grayson? Carter Grayson of Grayson Enterprises?" John asked.

"Yeah. Do you know him?"

"No. We know of him," John spoke. "He owns half of New York City."

"I've heard he's not a very nice man," Scott spoke. "His father owned a small mom and pop real estate company that was going under. After his father passed away, Carter took over, turned it around in a matter of months, and expanded from selling homes to buying and selling properties. He has the biggest real estate company in all of New York. I'm sorry to hear about his sister."

"She's young and she's dying. But, unlike her brother, she has a lightness that washes over her. His aura is just all darkness." I sighed. "I'm going to go upstairs, take a bath, and get packed."

"Okay, sweetheart. We'll see you in the morning before you leave," John spoke.

I went to my room, started the water for a bath, and then pulled my suitcase from the closet. I couldn't stop my mind from thinking about Carter and the way he rudely dismissed my hand when I introduced myself. How could someone be so rude? But as rude as he was, it didn't take away the fact that he was so damn sexy. Living in the same house with him was going to be a challenge. I already knew it. He didn't like me and I needed to prepare myself for the abuse he was going to throw my way.

The next morning after getting dressed, I dragged my suitcase down the stairs and set it by the front door. Walking into the kitchen, I smiled as the aroma of my father's crepes filled the air.

"Good morning, pumpkin," my father Scott spoke.

"Morning, Dad." I kissed his cheek. "Where's Dad?"

"He had an emergency at the hospital. He told me to give you a big hug and kiss for him before you left. He felt bad not being able to stick around and say goodbye."

"It's okay. He has lives to save."

I poured myself a cup of coffee and took a seat at the island where a plate of crepes was waiting for me. My dad plated his and took the seat next to mine. After we talked and finished breakfast, there was a knock on the door. Upon answering it, a man who was about fifty years of age stood tall and proud in his black suit in front of me.

"Miss Benson, I presume?" he spoke.

"You must be Juan." I held out my hand.

He gave me a slight nod as he placed his hand in mine and lightly shook it.

"Are you ready to leave?" he asked.

"Yes. Here's my suitcase. I'll be out in a minute."

"Very well." He smiled.

I walked back into the kitchen and hugged my dad goodbye.

"I'll miss you, pumpkin."

"I'll miss you too. But you and Dad can come visit."

"We definitely will. Stay in touch. At least once a day." He kissed my head and walked me to the door.

"I will." I smiled.

Juan seemed nice. A lot nicer than his boss, Mr. Carter Grayson. I sat in the back of the black Bentley while he drove me to Carter and Nora's Fifth Avenue penthouse. When he pulled up to the curb, I climbed out and he grabbed my suitcase.

"I'll bring this up for you," he spoke.

"No need." I grabbed it from his hand. "I can do it. Thank you for picking me up and driving me here."

"You're very welcome, Miss Benson." He nodded.

"It's Zoey, Juan. Just Zoey." I smiled as I wheeled my suitcase through the double doors that Joseph held open for me.

"Good to see you again, Zoey." He tipped his hat.

"Good to see you too, Joseph. Have a good day."

"You too." He grinned.

I took the elevator up to the Grayson penthouse, and as soon as the doors opened, I stepped onto the exquisite black and white marbled flooring and took in a deep breath. This was going to be my home for the next couple of months.

"Hello," an older woman with auburn hair pulled back into a bun spoke. "You must be Miss Benson, Nora's nurse."

"Yes, I'm Zoey." I extended my hand to her.

"I'm Sadie, Mr. Grayson's housekeeper. I'll show you to your room."

I followed her down the hallway and followed her into the room next to Nora's. It was stunning. Solid hardwood floor with a chevron pattern greeted me as well as the gray-colored walls. A canopied bed dressed in white was the focal point of the room. The view was spectacular from the floor-to-ceiling windows that overlooked Madison Square Park. In front of the windows was a window seat made of white buttoned material that would make the perfect spot to cuddle up and read a book or stare out into the New York City night.

"This is exquisite," I spoke. "Is Nora in her room?"

"Yes. She's sleeping right now. If you need anything, just let me know."

"Thank you, Sadie."

"You're welcome, Zoey. I hope you enjoy your stay."

"I think I will as long as Mr. Grayson isn't around." I smirked.

She let out a light laugh. "He can be a little tough to be around sometimes."

Sadie left the room and I began to unpack my suitcase. Once I was finished, I stepped into Nora's room and found she was awake.

"Good morning." I smiled.

She held her hand out to me. "Good morning. Welcome to Casa Grayson."

"Thank you." I placed my hand in hers. "Did you have breakfast yet?"

"I ate a small amount." She lightly smiled. "It looks like it's a beautiful day outside."

"It is. There's just a light breeze and not a cloud in the sky. Unfortunately, we won't have too many more of these days."

"I want to go to Central Park," she softly spoke.

"Okay. Let's get you ready, then."

Once I helped Nora get ready, I wheeled her down to the lobby where her driver, Frank, was waiting for us.

"Frank, this is my new nurse, Zoey. Zoey, this is Frank."

"Nice to meet you, Zoey." He smiled as he lightly shook my hand.

"Nice to meet you too."

I helped Nora into the car while Frank folded up her wheelchair and put it in the trunk. Once we arrived at the location Nora requested, I wheeled her to the Conservatory Gardens.

"There's a bench over there under the archway." She pointed.

Once I wheeled her over and helped her from her chair and onto the bench, I took a seat beside her.

"This place gives me so much peace," she spoke.

"It's beautiful here." I smiled.

"I'm sorry if my brother was an ass to you."

"Don't worry about it. He certainly is a grumpy man." I laughed.

"He's not like that all the time." She looked over at me. "Hell, who am I kidding, he is like that all the time. I just don't want him to scare you off or something."

Placing my hand on hers, I spoke, "He won't. I'm here to take care of and help you, not him."

"I don't have much time left on this earth and he's having a hard time dealing with it. I'm going to need you to help him get through it. Can you do that, Zoey?" she asked.

Her concern for her brother touched me. She was putting him first before herself.

"Of course I'll try to help him get through it. But I can only do that if he allows it."

"He won't, but you'll have to try. Please promise me you'll try." She squeezed my hand.

"Yes, of course I will."

"Thank you."

We talked for a bit more and then I wheeled her around so she could touch and smell the beautiful flowers that surrounded the area. This garden was a sacred place and I knew why she felt so peaceful here. We spent a couple hours in Central Park and then she asked to go home for she was exhausted.

When we got home, I helped her into bed, gave her the medications she needed to take and waited until she fell asleep.

Chapter Five

Carter

After I left the office and arrived home, I found Zoey sitting at the island eating the dinner Sadie prepared.

"Where's Nora?" I asked as I set my briefcase down.

"Hello there." Zoey smiled. "How was your day?"

"It doesn't matter how my day was. How is Nora doing today?" I snapped at her.

"She's sleeping."

"Did she eat?"

"She ate a little bit. We went to Central Park earlier for a couple of hours."

"Why did you do that?" I asked as I poured myself a scotch.

"Because she wanted to go."

"And do you really think it's a good idea that she leaves the house? What if she catches something? Her immune system is weak and you of all people should know that," I spoke with irritation.

"The risk is high, but she knows that. It's good for her to spend some time outside this house."

"Even if it kills her?"

"She's dying, Mr. Grayson. What part of that do you not understand?"

I glared at her. *How dare she.*

"Your job is to take care of Nora, not make me understand what the fuck is going on. I'm fully aware she's dying."

"My job is to not only take care of the patient, but to also help the family get through it."

I downed the last drop of my scotch and slammed the glass on the counter.

"I don't need your help, Miss Benson. Not now, not ever." I pointed at her.

"You need more help than you realize," she spewed.

"What's going on in here?" Nora asked as she wheeled herself into the kitchen. "Carter, I could hear you yelling from my room. Why are you yelling at her?"

I walked over and kissed her forehead.

"I'm not yelling. Now if you'll excuse me, I need to go get changed. I'm going out tonight."

"I don't want you to go out. I want you home with me," she spoke and I froze in place.

"I've already made plans, Nora," I softly spoke.

"You always have plans, Carter."

"I have a life too. I'll stay in tomorrow night. I promise," I spoke as I walked out of the kitchen and headed up to my room.

After changing my clothes, I went downstairs and asked Zoey to come to my office.

"I want to make sure you stored my phone number in case of an emergency, and I want you to clear it with me before you leave this house with Nora."

"Yes, Mr. Grayson. I have your number stored and I will clear it with you before leaving the house with your sister."

"That'll be all, Miss Benson."

She gave me a light nod, and as she began to leave my office, she turned to me.

"It's Zoey, Mr. Grayson. Just Zoey."

I swallowed hard as she walked out. Looking at her number in my phone, I sent her a text message.

"For emergencies only."

"Of course," she replied.

There was something about that girl that irritated me, but I couldn't put my finger on why. She irritated me in Starbucks and now she irritated me in my own home. I needed to get a grip. She was here for Nora. Staying away from her would be in both our best interest.

****

Zoey

Nora confided in me about her brother's excessive going out and how much it bothered her. She accused him of running away from reality and hiding in the depths of sex and booze.

"Who's Angelique?" I asked her.

She looked at me with wide eyes. "Did Carter mention her name to you?"

"No." I shook my head.

"Then how do you know that name?"

"She told me."

"Angelique told you?" Her eye narrowed at me.

"Yes."

"That's impossible. Angelique is dead."

"I know she is."

"Zoey, you're kind of freaking me out right now. Angelique was Carter's fiancée before she died five years ago."

"They were going to have a son," I spoke.

"Yes, she was pregnant." A look of shock splayed across her face.

I gently smiled. "He looks just like Mr. Grayson."

"How do you know all this? It isn't possible."

"I have a gift, Nora. Is that the reason your brother is the way he is?"

"Yeah, pretty much. When I was eighteen and he was twenty, our mother passed away from cancer. It was really hard on our dad and he couldn't recover. A year after her death, he committed suicide to end his pain and suffering. Then, Carter met Angelique and she was the love of his life. A couple years later, she got pregnant and he proposed. They were going to wait until after the baby was born to get married. She was at a crosswalk waiting to cross the street, and when the signal turned for her, she started walking and a drunk driver came flying around the corner and hit her. The paramedics said that she only lived a few minutes after she was hit. They rushed her to the hospital to try and save the baby, but by time they got there, it was too late. Please, don't ever tell him I told you this. He doesn't talk about it at all. In fact, he went to great lengths to keep it out of the press when it happened. After that, he changed. He just wasn't the same. Now I'm dying and he can't handle it. In his thirty years of life, he has experienced way too much death with the people who meant the most to him." Tears formed in her eyes.

"He's in a dark place, Nora. His energy is very dark."

"I know, and I've tried to help him, but I can't. I can't die until I know he's going to be okay."

I reached over and grabbed hold of her hand.

"Everything will be okay. He will be okay. I promise."

Who was I to make a promise like that? Sure, everything would be okay for her in the afterlife, but for Carter, he would forever be imprisoned in his own personal hell. A hell he chose to stay buried in without any attempt to break free. A place where he felt safe from the turbulence and unfairness of his life. After tucking Nora into bed and making sure she was comfortable, I went into my room and attempted to turn on the TV, but it didn't seem to work. So, I grabbed a bottle of water from the fridge and sat down on the couch in the living room. At about midnight, I heard the elevator doors open, so I quickly turned off the TV and went into my room.

I could hear his footsteps down the hallway and then they stopped at Nora's room. A few moments later, the footsteps started again down the hallway, then stopped. Climbing into bed, I settled myself into a comfortable position. It wasn't too long after that, I heard the faint sound of music playing. I lay there and tried to listen, but I couldn't make out what song it was. Why was he playing music at this time of night?

I climbed out of bed and quietly walked out of my room and down the hallway where the music was coming from. Stopping at his office door, which was slightly ajar, I carefully peeked inside. Carter sat there in his chair with a drink in one hand and a picture in the other while the song *Unchained Melody* played quietly in the room. I couldn't stop staring at him as he stared at that picture in complete despair and agony.

Chapter Six

Zoey

A week had passed and his attitude toward me was still the same. Bitterness, anger, and hate consumed him. He was broken. So broken that merely existing was what he'd become accustomed to. The one thing he didn't understand was that we were all broken in one way or another. Yet through all the jagged edges of the pieces that made him up, he was still strangely beautiful.

Nora had Sadie prepare a special dinner for the three of us. Carter had agreed to stay in and she wanted me to join them. I felt unsure because I knew he wouldn't approve of it. It was six o'clock when he stepped off the elevator and made his way into the kitchen. He mumbled a hello to me and then walked over to Nora and kissed her head.

"How are you today?" he asked her.

"I'm fine. I had Sadie prepare dinner for us."

"Good. I'm starving."

"Zoey will be joining us," she spoke to him.

"I see." He glanced over at me.

"It's okay, Nora. I'll go to my room so you and your brother can have some time alone."

"Don't be silly. We want you to join us. Don't we, Carter?" she spoke through gritted teeth.

"If she feels more comfortable in her room——"

"Carter!" Nora loudly voiced.

"Please, join us, Zoey. It would be ridiculous for you to eat in your room," he spoke.

"It's okay, really. I don't mind."

"Enough with the arguing. Nora wants you to sit with us and so you shall. Understood?" His brow arched.

"Sure. Fine." I lightly smiled. "If you insist."

I helped Nora from her wheelchair into a seat at the table and then took my seat next to her while Carter sat across from me.

"Tell us about your family, Zoey," Nora spoke. "So far since you've been here, I never really asked you about them."

"I have two dads who have raised me since I was a baby."

"Your parents are gay?" Carter asked as he picked up his fork.

"Yes. I was left on the stairs of the church they attended," I lied.

"Oh my god, you poor thing. So you never had a mother?" Nora pouted.

"No." I gave a small smile. "But, John and Scott, are the best parents anyone could ever ask for. They gave me a good life."

"Do you still live with them?" Carter asked.

"I do. Right now it doesn't make sense to get my own place since I'm not home much, with my job and everything."

"I guess that makes sense," he spoke.

"What do your parents do?" Carter asked.

"John is a doctor who works in the ER and Scott is a firefighter."

"Nice." Nora slowly nodded. "I'd love to meet them."

"They come to the city a lot. Maybe we can have lunch with them one day."

"I'd like that." She smiled. "Or maybe we can have them over for dinner."

"No. I don't think so," Carter spoke.

"Why?" Nora asked him.

"Because Zoey is the hired help. We don't need to have her family over to the house."

"Wow, Carter." Nora looked at him in disgust.

Was I surprised he said that? No. It fit his demeanor. I brushed it off and took my plate to the kitchen. When I returned to the dining room, Nora asked if I could help her with a bath. After getting her settled into bed, I walked back out to the dining room to finish cleaning up. As I was loading the dishwasher, I became startled when I turned around and saw Carter standing there staring at me.

"Shit, you scared me!"

"What are you doing?" he asked.

"Cleaning up from dinner." I gave him an odd look.

"Why? That's what I have a housekeeper for."

"You can't let these dishes sit out all night," I spoke.

"Whatever, but don't expect a bonus or anything in your check because you chose to clean up." He began to walk away.

"Wait!" I yelled.

He stopped and turned to look at me.

"I don't expect anything extra, especially from you. I'm doing this because it's the right thing to do. But someone like you wouldn't know anything about that." I pointed my finger at him.

He had finally broken me. His attitude towards me and his verbal abuse finally sent me over the edge.

"Are you finished?" His brow arched.

"I have more to say, but for the fear of losing my job, I'll just keep my mouth shut."

He cocked his head and folded his arms. God, how I wished he wasn't so handsome.

"No. Go ahead. Tell me more."

"Just leave me alone, Mr. Grayson. Please let me finish cleaning up and then I'll head to my room." I turned and put the last dish in the dishwasher.

"Fine." He stormed out of the kitchen.

After wiping down the counters, I retreated to my room, where I called my dad, John.

"Hey, sweetheart, how's the job going?"

"That man is unbearable!"

A light laugh came from the other end.

"You mean Carter Grayson?"

"Yes. He's so rude and mean. I try to be nice, but with him, it's becoming impossible."

"Just remember why you're there, Zoey. Don't let someone like him distract you from what's really important."

"I know, Dad." I sighed.

"What's going on with you? You never let anyone get to you like this."

He was right. I always saw the good in everyone and never reacted like this. I knew Carter was hurting and I saw the pain in his eyes every single day, but I still struggled with his behavior.

"Nothing is going on with me. He's just annoying."

There was a brief moment of silence on the other end.

"Are you sure you're not developing some sort of feelings for him?" he asked.

"Dad, he's a mean and miserable person. How could anyone develop feelings for someone like him?"

"Okay, sweetheart, just checking."

Just as I ended the call, I heard Carter scream my name from Nora's room. Throwing down my phone, I ran in there to see what was wrong.

"Shit, she's having a seizure!" I pushed Carter out of the way so I could help her. "Has she had a seizure before?" I asked.

"No!"

"Call 911."

As soon as her seizure calmed, I rolled her on her side to keep her airways open.

"You're going to be okay, Nora. Just try to relax and breathe normal."

"I'm so tired," she softly spoke.

"I know. Just relax. An ambulance is on the way to take you to the hospital."

"No." She shook her head. "No hospital."

I reached over and grabbed her hand.

"This is your first seizure. You need to go. It's not a choice and I'll be there with you." I turned and looked at Carter to make sure he was okay. He was as pale as a ghost. "Are you okay?" I asked him.

"I'm fine," he spoke with a shaky voice.

Not too long after Carter called, the paramedics arrived, put Nora on the stretcher, and transported her to the hospital. I rode with her in the back while Carter had Juan drive him separately. Once we arrived at the ER, they rushed Nora back and told me and Carter to sit in the waiting room. He took a seat in a chair with his elbows rested on his knees and his hands covering his face. I had a feeling we were going to be there for a while, so I grabbed two cups of coffee from the machine in the waiting room and handed one to him.

"Here, I thought you could use this."

He looked up at the coffee and then at me.

"Thanks." He took it from my hand.

"I didn't know how you took it, so I just got black," I spoke.

"Black is fine."

Chapter Seven

Carter

Seeing Nora like that scared the living shit out of me and I never wanted to see it again.

"Thank you, Zoey," I spoke.

"For what?"

"For taking care of Nora."

"It's my job, Mr. Grayson."

She was right, it was her job. But I still felt the need to thank her. She sat across from me, and as I stared at her, she wouldn't even make eye contact. I needed to talk to her because I just couldn't sit and let my mind overthink the worst. It drove me insane.

"How do you do it?" I asked. "How do you surround yourself with so much pain and death all the time?"

She brought her cup up to her lips and took a sip from it.

"This is what I was born to do," she simply said with a small smile.

Just as I was about to ask her what she meant, a doctor walked into the waiting room.

"For Nora Grayson?"

We both stood up as the doctor walked over to us.

"Nora is resting now. We did a brain scan and saw a shadow in another area. Seizures are common with this stage of cancer. It was to be expected, to be honest. We've started her on fluids and some medication. I want to keep her here for a couple of days just to monitor her and get an MRI. You may go see her but not for too long. She needs her rest."

"Thank you, doctor," I spoke.

Zoey and I followed the doctor behind the double doors and down the hallway where Nora was.

"We're going to be moving her upstairs to room 205 as soon as it's ready," the doctor spoke. "Like I said, don't stay too long."

I gave him a nod as he walked out of the room. Zoey stood on one side of her bed while I walked around to the other side.

"She looks so peaceful," I spoke as I stared at my sister.

"The seizure took a toll on her body. She's resting comfortably now."

I could hear the sounds of an old woman a couple of curtains down moaning and yelling out. It was constant and it really irritated me. Just when I'd had about enough, a nurse walked in and took Nora's vitals.

"Can't you do something about that woman?" I asked the nurse. "It's very disruptive, not only to family members but also the other patients here."

"She's been like that all day. We can't calm her down and the medication doesn't seem to be working. We're waiting for a room to open up on the psychiatric floor so we can transfer her up there."

"Does she have any family?" Zoey asked.

"Her neighbor brought her in and said that she has no family that she knew of."

After checking Nora's vitals, the nurse left and Zoey followed behind.

"Where are you going?" I asked her.

"I'll be right back." She smiled.

I was curious as to what she was up to, so I followed her out of the room and down the hall where the old woman lay yelling and moaning. Zoey stood at her bedside and took hold of her hand. The old woman looked at her and instantly quieted down.

"It's okay. It's time for you to go home," Zoey whispered.

The old woman looked at her and then turned her head to the other side and blankly stared at nothing.

"See. They're waiting for you," Zoey spoke. "There's nothing to be afraid of. They're here to take you home."

The old woman looked over at Zoey again and brought her hand up to her cheek.

"It's okay. I promise." Zoey smiled as she removed the woman's hand from her cheek and held it.

A gurgling noise erupted from her, and in an instant, she was gone. I stood there and watched as Zoey stared straight ahead with a smile on her face. I furrowed my brows as I looked at her. Swallowing hard, I turned around and went back to Nora's room. I didn't know what to make of what I'd just witnessed. Zoey walked back in the room just as Nora opened her eyes. We stayed with her until they transferred her up to room 205 and visiting hours had ended. As we walked out of the hospital and climbed into the car, I looked at her and spoke, "What the hell happened back there with that old woman?"

"She was dying but afraid to let go, so I helped her. It's what I do, Mr. Grayson."

I shook my head in confusion.

"I heard you tell her that it was time to go home. Why would you lie to her like that?"

The corners of her mouth curved up into a small smile.

"I didn't lie to her. She was being called to go home, but she was too afraid."

"I take it you're not talking about her home here?" I asked as I narrowed my eye.

"No. She was being called to go home to Heaven."

"And you really believe that load of shit?"

"It's not a load of shit, and yes, I do."

I sat there, staring out the passenger window shaking my head. This woman was insane.

"It is a load of shit. There's no such place and there certainly is no God. Believe what you want and live in your fucking fairytale world," I spewed. "But don't ever talk to me about it."

Chapter Eight

Zoey

I sat there in disbelief of the hatred that had just come from his mouth. My first response should have been to tell him what a mean and horrible person he was. But I didn't. I kept my mouth shut. He may not have believed in God or Heaven, but he sure did believe in Hell because that was where his soul was held captive. He glanced over at me, waiting for me to respond, but I wouldn't give him the satisfaction.

Juan pulled up to the curb of Carter's apartment building and we both climbed out. Following behind him, we stepped onto the elevator and took it up to his penthouse. As soon as the doors opened, he stormed out, went into his office, and slammed the door shut.

I was hungry, so I went into the kitchen and pulled an apple out of the refrigerator. Taking a small bowl down from the cupboard, I set it on the counter and began cutting the apple into thin slices.

"Why?" I asked as I looked up at the ceiling. "Why did you have to put him in my path?"

I sighed as I sliced another piece, but instead of cutting the apple, I cut my finger.

"Shit!" I screamed as I threw down the knife.

Grabbing a napkin that was sitting next to me, I tightly wrapped it around my finger. The stinging, throbbing, and overall pain was a little too much. I took in a long, deep breath.

"What happened?" I heard Carter ask as he stepped into the kitchen.

"I cut my finger. It's no big deal."

"It looks like a big deal to me since that napkin is soaked in blood."

"I said it's no big deal, Mr. Grayson," I spoke as I tried to walk past him.

He reached out and lightly grabbed my arm.

"Please sit down so I can take a look at it. You may need stitches."

"I don't need stitches. I'm a nurse. I would know if I need stitches."

"Just sit so I can take a look."

I sighed as I sat down on the stool at the island. Carter took the seat next to me and carefully unwrapped the napkin from my finger.

"Wow. You really did a number on this. I think you need stitches," his calm voice spoke.

"All I need is a butterfly bandage. Do you have any?" I asked.

"I don't know. I'll have to go check. Don't move from this spot. I'll be right back."

He reached for another napkin and wrapped it around my finger. Something happened when he touched my hand. Something I couldn't explain. It was like lightning flowed through me. The same lightning I'd only experienced one other time in my life. I stayed seated on the stool and waited for him to come back. A few moments later, he returned with a first aid kit.

"I found this kit in the bathroom. Maybe there's a butterfly bandage in here," he spoke as he opened it.

Rummaging through the kit, he pulled out a butterfly bandage.

"Found one." He held it up. "But first we need to clean the wound out."

He wrapped his hand around my wrist and led me to the sink. I didn't say a word. I just let him take control, which he was good at. He unwrapped the napkin and stuck my finger under the slow stream of water. I bit down on my bottom lip at the sharp pain that radiated through me.

"I know it hurts, but we have to clean it," he spoke.

He pulled a piece of paper towel off the roll, carefully dried my finger, and then wrapped a piece of gauze around it.

"Hold this gauze on it while I open up the packet of ointment and the bandage."

I did as he asked and watched while he opened the small packet of antibiotic ointment.

"Remove the gauze."

After finishing up with the ointment, he placed the butterfly bandage around my finger.

"There." The corners of his mouth slightly, and I mean very slightly, curved upwards.

I nearly fell to the ground because that was the first time I'd ever seen somewhat of a smile cross his lips. I didn't think he could get any sexier than he already was, but at that moment, his sexy level went up one hundred percent.

"Thank you," I softly spoke.

"You're welcome. I know I don't need to tell you that you should take some Motrin for the pain, right?"

"No, you don't have to tell me. I know."

"Good. It's late. You should get some rest," he spoke as he placed his hand on my shoulder.

I gave him a small smile and went to my bedroom. His attentiveness was a little overwhelming since he hadn't shown that side of himself from the day I met him. Maybe there was something or someone beneath all the darkness that enshrouded him.

I awoke around one a.m. and my finger was throbbing, so I climbed out of bed and headed to the kitchen for some more Motrin and a glass of water. As I stumbled down the hall in a sleepy daze, I stopped outside Carter's office where I heard the same song as the other night play.

Carter

I sat behind my desk and stared at the picture of Angelique while her favorite song played and I sipped my scotch. I tormented myself with this nightly ritual believing that somehow, she'd come back to me. I missed her and I couldn't let go. I had everything. I had it all. A multi-billion-dollar company, a woman I loved, and a baby on the way. I was going to have my own family. One I could protect and keep safe from the harm and damage of the world. But I failed. I failed with my parents, Angelique, my son, and now with Nora. Even with all the money in the world, I couldn't save any of them.

When the song ended, I tucked the picture safely away in my desk and poured another glass of scotch. As I sat there, I thought about Zoey. Not only about her cutting her finger, but about what happened at the hospital. That old woman was a total mess until Zoey walked in and talked to her. She reminded me of— I quickly got the thought out of my head, set my glass down, and walked out of my office.

"Jesus, Zoey. You scared me. What are you doing up?" I asked as I practically ran into her.

"I needed some more Motrin. Why are you still up?"

"I just finished doing some work. I'm heading up to bed now. Sleep well."

"Thanks. You too."

As I headed up the stairs, I looked down at my semi-hard cock. Seeing her in that nightshirt put all kinds of ideas in my head. Ideas that shouldn't have been there. I climbed into bed and exhaustion overtook me. Laying my head on the pillow, I couldn't stop thinking about the feeling that emerged inside me when I touched Zoey, and it posed a great problem for me.

Chapter Nine

Zoey

I climbed out of bed and got dressed before heading to the kitchen for some coffee.

"Good morning, Sadie," I spoke.

"Good morning, Zoey. What happened to your finger?"

"It's just a cut. I was slicing an apple last night and missed."

"It's more than just a cut. Don't let her fool you. It looked like a murder scene in here last night." Carter grinned as he walked in.

Two days, two smiles. It was in my best interest not to get too used to him doing that.

"You two go sit down and I'll pour you some coffee," Sadie spoke.

I took a seat at the island next to Carter and he glanced over at me.

"How did you sleep?" he asked.

"Not too bad. How about you?"

"It doesn't matter. I didn't ask you so you could ask about me," he rudely spoke.

And he's back.

"I'm heading over to the hospital before the office. Are you coming or not?"

"I have a couple things to do before heading over there. I'll just take a cab," I replied.

"Suit yourself." He drank his coffee and got up from the stool. "Have a good day, Sadie. I'll see you when I get home," he spoke.

"You too, Mr. Grayson." She glanced over at me.

As soon as he walked out of the kitchen, I did the unthinkable. I held up my middle finger in his direction. Sadie laughed.

"He's such an asshole," I spoke as I brought my cup up to my lips.

"Yes I am. I'm surprised it took you this long to realize that." He popped his head around the wall of the kitchen and glared at me.

I gulped because I didn't think he could hear me.

"Oh my god," I mouthed silently to Sadie.

She smiled and made me some eggs before I headed out the door.

Before going to the hospital, I stopped by the florist. As I stood in front of the cooler and stared at the vast variety of colorful flowers, I smiled as a memory that would never be forgotten filled my head.

"Is there something I can help you with?" a nice young girl spoke as she approached me.

"Could you make me up a colorful bouquet of flowers?"

"Of course. Any specific flowers you would like me to use?"

"Just ones that are colorful and bright." I smiled.

"Would you like them in a vase?"

"Yes, please. I'm taking them over to the hospital."

As soon as the arrangement was ready and paid for, I hailed a cab and headed to the hospital. When I walked into Nora's room, I was surprised that Carter was still there.

"Zoey." Nora smiled. "Oh my gosh, what beautiful flowers."

"How are you feeling?" I asked as I set them down on the table next to her.

"Tired."

"Hello, Zoey," Carter spoke in a low voice.

"Ah. I'm good enough to say hello to but not goodbye?" I cocked my head at him.

His eye narrowed at me for a moment with a look of disapproval. But I didn't care. I was no longer going to let him disrespect and treat me the way he had been.

"I need to go." He leaned over and kissed Nora's forehead. "I'll stop by later, on my way home."

"Okay." She smiled.

As he began to walk out the door, I spoke, "Goodbye, Mr. Grayson."

He turned and looked at me for a brief moment and then continued out the door. Silence never left his lips.

"What the hell is going on between the two of you?" Nora asked.

"Your brother is a rude, pompous ass," I spoke as I took the seat Carter sat in.

"I know he is and I told you why he's like that. What happened to your finger?"

"I cut it last night slicing an apple. Actually, your brother walked in right after it happened and took control. He cleaned it up and put this butterfly over it."

"Really? He did that?"

"Yes. I thought maybe I had witnessed a breakthrough, but he was back to his normal self this morning."

"The way he is, Zoey, isn't his normal self. Carter used to be an amazing loving person and he was so full of life. He didn't have a mean bone in his body. This change I've witnessed for the past five years is so incomprehensible to me and it breaks my heart. He became a victim of circumstance." She began to close her eyes.

Gently placing my hand on hers, I spoke, "Get some rest and I'll see you later."

As I was leaving the hospital, my phone rang and it was Holly.

"Hello," I answered.

"Hey there, bestie. I'm in the city today. Any chance we can meet up somewhere for a bit?"

"Actually, I can meet you now. Nora is in the hospital. She had a seizure last night."

"Is she okay?"

"She's doing better today, but they want to keep her overnight again just to monitor her and do a couple more scans. How about Starbucks on Fifth Avenue?"

"Sounds good. I can be there in about ten minutes."

"Great. I'll see you soon."

Just as I climbed out of the cab, I saw Holly walking down the street. We hugged and headed inside. After ordering our coffee, we took a seat at a small table for two by the window.

"So, how are you? How are things going with Mr. Mean?"

"He's unbearable. He's miserable. He's a rude, pompous ass. Need I go on?" I smiled.

"Umm. No. I think you just covered it." She laughed. "Want to know what I think about the situation?"

"What?"

"I think you like him." She smiled.

Laughter escaped my lips.

"No, I don't. How could you even say that after what I just said about him?"

"Because I've known you my whole life, Zoey, and you never let anyone get to you. You always defended the mean girls in school. So your reaction, this out-of-character reaction to Carter Grayson, is telling me you're into him."

Damn her.

I ended up telling Holly what I knew about Carter's past, all the death he experienced, and how he didn't believe in God or Heaven.

"Wow. Now I have a better understanding why he's the way he is. How sad."

"I know, but he can't take it out on people. The anger that consumes him is frightening," I spoke.

"Then make him see there is a Heaven and a God. You of all people can do that."

"I can't force someone to believe something they aren't ready for or don't want to accept."

"I suppose." She shrugged.

After a couple hours of talking, it was time to head back to the hospital to check on Nora. When I arrived, I saw Carter heading to the elevator.

"Shit," I mumbled.

He stepped inside and the doors began to shut. I could either wait for the elevator to come back down or I could yell for him to hold them. Knowing him, he'd probably push the close button just to prevent me from getting on.

"Hold on," I shouted as I walked quickly to the elevator.

He put his hand in between and stopped the doors from closing.

"Thank you," I spoke as I stepped inside.

"You're welcome." He glanced over at me.

When the doors opened, I stepped out first and walked ahead of him. When I got to Nora's room, she wasn't in there, so I went to look for her nurse.

"Do you know where Nora Grayson is?" I asked.

"She's having an MRI. She should be done in a few minutes."

"Ah, okay. Thanks."

I walked back to the room and found Carter sitting in the chair.

"Well, where is she?" he asked.

"Having an MRI. She should be done in a few minutes."

He didn't respond as he pulled out his phone and started looking at it.

Okay then, jerk.

I stared out the window and felt a twinge in my finger. When I looked down, the bandage came loose, the cut opened, and blood started to drip down my hand.

"Shit," I spoke as I went over to the sink and wrapped a piece of paper towel around my finger.

"What's wrong?" Carter asked. "Is it your finger again?"

"When Nora gets here, tell her I'll be right back. I need to go to the ER."

I took the elevator down to the ER and approached the receptionist at the desk.

"Please sign in and have a seat," she spoke.

"This is a little bit of an emergency." I held up my blood-soaked finger.

"Oh dear. Let's get you back into a room."

I followed her to room three and took a seat on the bed. After giving her my name, a nurse walked in and examined my finger.

"Ouch. Did this just happen?" she asked.

"I did it last night. I butterflied it, but it just came loose."

She opened the drawer and took out a piece of thick gauze and wrapped it around my finger.

"The doctor will be in shortly." She smiled.

I knew too well what that meant in an ER. I would bleed to death before I saw a doctor. I sat there and looked around the room. I slowly closed my eyes and the memories came flooding back as if it happened just yesterday.

"Pumpkin, what happened?" my dad John spoke as he entered the room.

"Dad? What are you doing here?" I asked in confusion.

"They were short staffed today, so Ed called and asked if I could fill in. It just so happened I was off from St. Francis today. I was going to call you later and see if you could join me for dinner. Now what happened?" he asked as he removed the gauze.

"I cut it last night while I was slicing an apple."

"You're a nurse, Zoey. You knew this needed to be stitched." He cocked his head at me.

"I was hoping the butterfly would close it up. I really didn't think it was that bad. Nora is here. The ambulance brought her in last night."

"Why?" he asked as he numbed my finger.

"She had a seizure."

As he began stitching my finger, I heard Carter's loud voice down the hallway.

Chapter Ten

Carter

"What you don't seem to understand, sweetheart, is that she's my employee and she's currently living at my house. So as far as I'm concerned, I have a right to check on her. There you are." I stopped in the doorway.

"Mr. Grayson, what are you doing?"

"I came to see what was going on."

The doctor turned around and gave me a smile.

"Come on in and have a seat. I'll be finished in a minute."

"Mr. Grayson, this is my father, John Benson. Dad, this is Carter Grayson."

"Your father?" I cocked my head.

"Yes. They asked him to fill in today. He's still on staff here on occasion. He used to work here before we moved to Connecticut."

"Ah. I see. Nice to meet you, Dr. Benson."

"Same here, Mr. Grayson." He nodded. "Okay, pumpkin. All done." He kissed her forehead. "My shift ends at six. Will you be available for dinner?"

"Yeah. Nora isn't being released until tomorrow."

"Great." He turned and looked at me. "If you don't have any plans, Mr. Grayson, why don't you join us?"

I glanced over at Zoey and saw the expression on her face. She didn't look happy that her father asked me to join them.

"Actually, I don't have any plans. I'd love to join you." I smirked. "In fact, why don't we just have dinner at my penthouse? My housekeeper is a wonderful cook."

"Isn't that a little short notice for Sadie?" Zoey asked.

"No." I arched my brow at her.

"Sounds good." John smiled.

"Are you ready to go see Nora now?" I asked.

She walked in front of me down the hall, and when we reached the elevator, she spoke, "Why?"

"Why what?" I placed my hands in my pants pockets.

"I'm the hired help, remember? You don't need to have my family over to your house. Why couldn't you just have said no?"

"I didn't have any plans for tonight, so why not?"

She glared at me as we stepped onto the elevator and took it up to Nora's floor. When we entered the room, the doctor was there talking to her. He placed his hand on hers and gave it a gentle squeeze before leaving the room.

"What was that all about?" I asked.

"There's another tumor and the cancer has spread."

A feeling of sickness took over me and I needed to sit down.

"Why don't you just have the chemo, sis? It can buy you some time," I spoke as I took hold of her hand.

"We've already talked about this and you said you supported my decision. I refuse to spend whatever life I have left sick as a dog from that fucking chemo! It's not going to cure me. You saw what it did to me the first time and I was stronger then."

"I do support your decision." I leaned over and kissed her forehead. "I'm sorry."

"I'm really tired now, so if you don't mind, I want to go to sleep. The doctor said he'll release me tomorrow at eight a.m., so I'll see you then," Nora spoke.

After saying our goodbyes, Carter and I headed back to his penthouse.

"I know how hard this is for you," Zoey spoke as we sat in the back of the car.

"Do you really?" I asked in a monotone voice as I glanced over at her.

"Yes. I do. I know you've been through a lot, Mr. Grayson."

"You don't know shit, Zoey. Unless Nora told you." I narrowed my eye at her.

"She told me a little, and I'm sorry for your loss."

Juan pulled up to the curb and I immediately got out of the car.

"And you expect me to believe there's a God," I spoke in anger as I entered the building.

"There is," she said as we stepped into the elevator.

I ignored her comment because if I had responded, I would have lost it, and that was something I didn't want to do.

The moment I stepped out of the elevator, I went over to the bar and poured myself a double scotch. Hearing that Nora's cancer had spread tore me apart more than I already was. I wasn't ready to lose her. Fuck, I'd never be ready. I downed my drink, set the glass on the bar, and headed upstairs to my bedroom to change my clothes before Zoey's father arrived.

As I was coming down the stairs, I heard John's and Zoey's voices in the foyer.

"Hello, John," I spoke as I extended my hand.

"Hello, Carter. Your penthouse is stunning."

"Thank you. Would you like a drink? Perhaps a scotch or a bourbon?"

"Scotch would be good."

I headed over to the bar and poured us each a drink.

"Would you like something, sweetheart?" John asked Zoey.

"I can get it myself, Dad," she spoke as she glared at me.

"Can I pour you a glass of wine?" I spoke as I glared back at her.

"I wouldn't want you to go to any trouble, Mr. Grayson. If you'll excuse me, I'm going to check on dinner."

I raised my brow at John and took a sip of my drink. Sadie announced that dinner was ready, so we headed into the dining room and took our seats.

"Sadie, this smells delicious." John smiled.

"Thank you, Dr. Benson. I hope you enjoy it."

"Sadie is the best cook in New York as far as I'm concerned," I spoke.

"Zoey isn't too bad herself. Isn't that right, sweetheart?" John spoke with a smile.

"Dad, stop."

"I must say, Carter, I'm highly impressed at your success at such a young age. Especially for dropping out of college."

"Dad!" Zoey exclaimed.

"It's fine, Zoey. That's public knowledge. Thank you, John. I had to drop out after my father passed away because we were on the verge of bankruptcy and his failing real estate business needed my attention.

"I'd say you are quite the genius for turning that company around and becoming the number one real estate mogul in New York in such a short period of time."

"Thank you. My company means everything to me. As I'm sure being a doctor means everything to you."

"It does. I love what I do and I love helping people."

Chapter Eleven

Zoey

Carter carried on a conversation with my dad as if they'd been old friends who hadn't seen each other in a long time. After we finished eating, my dad decided it was time to leave.

"I better get going. I have to be at the hospital tomorrow morning at six a.m. Thank you for dinner, Carter."

"You're welcome, John. Have a safe trip back to Connecticut."

"I will. Sweetheart, it was good to see you." He kissed my cheek. "Take care of that finger."

"I will, Dad. Be careful," I spoke as I walked him to the elevator. "Tell Dad I said hi and I miss him."

"He'll certainly be jealous once I tell him we had dinner together." He smiled.

Once the elevator door shut, I walked back to the living room and found Carter sitting on the couch with another glass of scotch.

"I'm going to go to my room for the night," I spoke.

He held up his glass and didn't say a word, basically saying that he didn't care. I sighed as I went to my room, shut the door, and changed into my pajamas. It was ten o'clock and I was getting ready to go to sleep for the night when I heard a loud noise coming from the kitchen. When I went to see what was going on, I found Carter on the floor in a drunken stupor with the bar stool knocked over.

"What is going on?" I asked as I bent down.

"The fucking stool was in the way," he slurred.

"Are you okay?" I asked as I grabbed his arm to help him up.

"I'm fine." He jerked out of my grip.

He tried to stand up, but he kept falling back.

"Please let me help you to bed," I spoke. "It's not going to kill you to take some help from me."

He glared at me and once again tried to get up, but couldn't. I sighed as I grabbed hold of his arm and helped him stand. Placing his arm around my neck, I guided him up the stairs as he stumbled quite a few times. I wanted to ask him why he drank so much, but I already knew. He was trying to drown his sorrows about Nora. Once we reached his bedroom, I helped him over to the bed and he fell back.

"Fuck," he spoke as he put his arm over his forehead.

"All you need is to sleep it off."

I bent down and removed his shoes and socks while he attempted to unbutton his shirt. He was failing, so I tried to help him. He grabbed my wrists and held them tight while his eyes burned into mine.

"Come closer," he spoke in a low voice.

I stared into his drunken eyes and brought my face closer to his. He let go of my wrists, softly stroked my cheek with his thumb, and then wrapped his hand around the nape of my neck and pulled me closer until our lips were mere inches from each other. I gulped and before I knew it, his lips were brushing against mine. The smell of liquor infiltrated my space while the taste of scotch fell upon my lips. This was wrong—wrong on many levels—but at the moment, I didn't care. It felt too good to pull away. Our tongues met as I placed my hands on each side of his face. Our lips moved in sync and his other hand made its way up my shirt. He groped my breast and let out a moan at the same time as sounds of pleasure escaped me. He rolled me over on my back and hovered over me as his tongue explored my neck. Suddenly, he stopped and rolled off me and onto his back.

"You need to go back to your room," he slurred as he placed his arm over his eyes.

Silence overtook me for a moment as I stared at him. I climbed off the bed, and before I walked out of his room, I spoke, "Sleep well, Mr. Grayson."

I climbed into bed, laid my head down and tucked my hands underneath my pillow. As I lay there, the tormenting events of just a few minutes ago haunted me. The softness of his scotch-stained lips against mine sent exhilarating vibrations down below. The feel of his hand on my breast made me tremble from head to toe, and the way his tongue explored my neck made me feel in such a way I'd never felt before. Ever. The brief sexual moment I experienced with Carter Grayson was unlike any other. Tomorrow would be awkward to say the least and I lay there and wondered if he would say anything about it at all.

I was up early so I could shower and get dressed before heading to the hospital to pick up Nora. I nervously walked into the kitchen and saw Sadie standing at the stove preparing some oatmeal. I let out a deep breath when I saw Carter wasn't there.

"Good morning, Sadie." I smiled as I poured myself a cup of coffee.

"Good morning, Zoey. Breakfast is almost ready."

"Thank you."

I took a seat on the stool and held the coffee cup with both hands wrapped around it.

"Have you seen Mr. Grayson yet?" I asked.

"No. Not yet. I'm sure he'll be down soon."

Sadie set my bowl of oatmeal down in front of me, and as I was eating, my phone dinged with a text message. Picking it up, I noticed it was from Carter.

"I'll be bringing Nora home in about a half hour."

I stared at his message in confusion. He was already gone and at the hospital?

"Apparently, Carter isn't here. He's at the hospital picking up Nora," I spoke to Sadie.

"Oh. I thought he was still home. I'll keep his oatmeal warm, then."

Before setting my phone down, I replied to his text.

"Okay."

I had assumed we'd pick Nora up together, but I guess there was no assuming anything where Mr. Carter Grayson was concerned. Nerves stirred inside me at the thought of seeing him after last night. I finished my oatmeal and took the last sip of my coffee when I heard the elevator ding and the doors open. Taking in a deep breath, I walked into the foyer.

"Welcome home." I smiled at Nora.

"Thanks, Zoey. It's good to be home."

"Are you hungry? Sadie made oatmeal."

"A little bit."

"I have to head to the office, Nora," Carter spoke as he bent down and kissed her cheek.

"Okay. I'll see you tonight," she softly spoke.

Carter stepped into the elevator without so much as looking at me. He either didn't remember what happened last night or he just didn't care. I wheeled Nora into the kitchen and over to the table then poured myself another cup of coffee.

"How did things go with Carter last night?" Nora asked as she slowly ate the oatmeal that Sadie thinned out for her.

"It went okay. He was just typical Carter."

"He got drunk last night, didn't he?"

"How did you know?" I asked.

"I could tell by his eyes and the fact that no matter how much cologne he put on, the smell of scotch was still on him."

I looked down and traced the rim of my coffee cup with my finger.

"He was pretty bad. He couldn't even stand up, so I helped him up to bed."

"I hate when he gets like that."

"Does he get drunk often?" I asked out of concern.

"Not as much as he used to, but he has his days. I can tell he likes you, Zoey."

"No he doesn't." I gave her a small smile as I sipped my coffee.

"I know my brother, and I see something in his eyes when he looks at you. Just like I see the same thing in your eyes when you look at him."

"Nora, I don't have—"

"Be patient with him, Zoey." She placed her hand on mine.

I gave her a tender smile and finished my coffee.

"I'm going to my room now," she spoke. "I have a phone call to make."

I got up from my seat and she put her hand up.

"I don't need help getting to my room. But if the phone call goes well, I'm going to need you to take me somewhere."

"You just came home from the hospital, Nora. You really shouldn't be going out today."

"I had a seizure and they kept me in that damn place to run some more tests. I'm fine."

She wheeled herself out of the kitchen and I looked at Sadie, who had the same look of despair on her face that I had on mine. After a few moments had passed, I heard Nora call my name. Walking into her room, I noticed she had grabbed her purse.

"I need you to take me to my attorney's office. It's only a couple of blocks from here."

"Okay. Are we going now?"

"Yes, and this little trip is to stay between us. Carter is never to know. Understand?"

"Of course." I nodded.

I helped her with her coat since the fall days were turning much cooler and we went down to the lobby. When Joseph saw us coming, he smiled and opened the door.

"You never saw us leave, Joseph," Nora spoke.

"Of course, Miss Grayson." He winked.

Chapter Twelve

Carter

I was sitting behind my desk trying to concentrate on work, but the only thing I could think of was how bad my head was hurting and what had happened last night between me and Zoey. I had to stop it from going any further because one, she was my employee, and two, it would be a mistake to have had sex with her in my drunken state. Even though I'd had sex plenty of times while I was drunk, Zoey was one woman who didn't deserve that. The one thing that I couldn't get out of my head was how she kissed me back. She didn't stop me, and had I kept going, it would have changed everything. She was beautiful and sexy, and my cock would have given anything to be buried deep inside her. For me, it was purely physical. The things she said and the things I'd witnessed were too much for me and I found it difficult to be around her. We were complete opposites. She voluntarily surrounded herself around death and illness, and I did everything I could to avoid it. She believed in Heaven and a God, and even though I once did, I didn't anymore, nor would I ever again.

"Excuse me, Mr. Grayson," my secretary, Breanna, spoke. "Mr. Cecil Campbell is on line one for you."

"Thank you, Breanna." I sighed as I picked up the phone. "Cecil, how are you?"

"Have you made your decision yet, Carter?"

"I have, and I've decided that you're going to sell me the property at the value we discussed."

"The price went up, Carter. I have others waiting in line behind you. All I have to do is give one of them a call and the property will be theirs tomorrow at the price I'm asking."

"You're bluffing. No one I know would be that stupid. What I do know is that the IRS is closing in to seize your property for your lack of tax payments over the last three years. And once they do that, I can actually pay a lower price for it. I'm trying to help you out, Cecil. Take what I've offered you and run with it. You know it's a damn good and fair price."

"I'll call you tomorrow, Carter." He hung up.

After setting the phone down, I opened my desk drawer and shook three aspirin into my hand. Just as I was about to head to a meeting, my cellphone rang. It was Nora.

"Is everything okay?" I asked.

"Yes. I need you to be home tonight. There's something I want to talk to you about."

"I'll be home around seven and we can talk then."

"Okay," she softly spoke.

I sighed as I ended the call and told Breanna to have Ross come into my office.

"What's up, Carter?"

"I just got off the phone with Cecil. He's going to sell the property for what we discussed. Get the contract drawn up."

"Excellent. By the way, how's the nurse working out?"

"Nora really likes her," I spoke.

"And you?"

"It doesn't matter what I think. As long as she provides my sister with the proper care, that's all that matters."

He stood there and stared at me with a narrowed eye.

"Yeah. You're right. I'll get moving on that contract."

Evening rolled around, and I left the office and headed home. I wasn't looking forward to seeing Zoey because I knew, at some point, we'd have to talk about what had happened last night. When I stepped off the elevator, I headed into the kitchen and found Zoey standing with the refrigerator open.

"Is Nora awake?" I asked, and she jumped.

"You scared me." She turned around and looked at me. "Can you please stop sneaking up on me?"

"I'm not sneaking up on you. You're obviously an easily frightened person. It must be all that death you surround yourself with."

"Yes, Nora is awake and she's waiting to talk to you."

"Do you know what it's about?" I asked.

"No. The only thing she said was that she wanted to speak to the both of us."

I sighed and set my briefcase down.

"Then we better go talk to her," I spoke.

The moment we stepped into Nora's room, she opened her eyes and looked at us.

"Good, you're home." She smiled. "Both of you, sit down."

I took a seat on the edge of the bed while Zoey took a seat in the chair.

"What did you want to talk about?" I asked as I lightly took hold of her hand.

"I don't have much longer, Carter. I can feel my body deteriorating. I want to spend what little time I have left at the beach house in Malibu."

"Nora." I shook my head. "That's not possible."

"It is possible, Carter, and this is my final wish. I want to sit on the beach, even if it is only for one day. I want to feel the ocean breeze and smell the salted air through my window as I lie in bed. It's getting colder here and I don't want to spend my final days in a dreary place."

"But, Nora, this is your home."

"So is the Malibu house."

"But—"

"Carter, this isn't about you. This is about me and my final wish."

I looked down and gulped because going back to that house was going to be the hardest thing I ever had to do. But she was right. This wasn't about me. I started to sweat at the thought because I knew once we left for California, I would return to New York alone.

"Okay," I whispered. "We'll leave in a couple of days. I have to get things settled at the office first, plus we'll need to pack."

"Thank you." She weakly squeezed my hand.

I looked over at Zoey, who sat there and didn't say a word.

"Can I see you in my office?" I asked her.

"Sure."

She followed me down the hallway and took a seat across from my desk.

"There are a couple things I want to discuss with you. First, about last night. I apologize for my actions. As you know, I was totally inebriated."

"I know and it's fine. Don't worry about it."

"It will never happen between us, Zoey. I want to make that very clear."

"You don't have to make that clear, Mr. Grayson, because I know it won't."

"Good. Now that we've gotten that out of the way, the second thing I want to discuss is California. Are you okay with going?"

"Yes. Of course I am. You seem hesitant about it. Why?"

"I am, but I'm doing it for Nora. The reason doesn't concern you. Understood?"

"Understood."

"The weather there is warm, so I'm assuming you'll have to go home and get some of your other clothes. Since I'm going to be home the rest of the night, I'll have Juan take you now and I'll keep an eye on Nora."

"Okay," she spoke.

"I don't think her traveling is a good idea. But what can I do? If she wants to spend what time she has left in Malibu, then who am I to try and stop her. That will be all. Juan will be waiting downstairs for you when you're ready."

She gave me a nod and walked out of my office. Picking up my phone, I called Sadie and asked her if she would like to come with us. Since it was only her and she didn't really have any family here, she accepted.

The thought of going back to that house terrified me. I wanted to sell it, but Nora wouldn't allow it, and I couldn't sell it without her permission since her name was also on the title. I got up from my desk and went over to the bar in the living room and poured myself a scotch. As I was about to drink it, I heard Zoey's voice.

"If you're going to drink while staying here alone with your sister, I'm not leaving."

"Excuse me?" I cocked my head at her.

"I'm sorry, Mr. Grayson, but after last night, I don't think I can trust you to be alone with her if you're drinking."

"Who the fuck do you think you are?" I set my glass down and walked over to her. "It's one drink and that's it."

"And one drink leads to many others. Especially with the state you're in about having to go to California. I know this is hard for you because you know you'll be coming back here without her, but drinking your problems away isn't going to help her or you."

I clenched my fist, which rested at my side, because I was one word away from massively exploding on her. I walked over to the bar, grabbed my glass, and dumped the scotch out.

"There. I won't have a drink until you return," I spoke in anger.

"Thank you." She turned and walked away.

Chapter Thirteen

Zoey

The tension between me and Carter was getting worse. I sat and watched his reaction when Nora told him she wanted to spend the rest of her time at their Malibu beach house. His face went pale, and before answering her, he swallowed hard. That place must have held a lot of memories. Not just memories of Nora, but of him and Angelique. He looked frightened and I'd wondered how long it had been since he'd been there.

When I arrived back home in Greenwich, my dads welcomed me with open arms, even if I was only there for a few minutes. As I was in my room, packing some of my clothes, both Scott and John sat on the edge of my bed.

"You're okay with this trip, right?" Scott asked.

"Of course." I smiled. "I go to where my job takes me. Their house is on the beach, so it'll be a nice change to get out of the city setting for a while."

"We'll miss you." John pouted.

"I'll miss both of you too. But we can facetime every day if you want. Well, I think that's all I'm bringing," I spoke as I looked down at my small suitcase.

Both of them walked me to the door and each hugged me tightly goodbye.

"Have a safe trip, sweetheart," John spoke.

"I will. I love you both very much."

"We love you too, baby." Scott kissed my head.

I returned to Carter's penthouse and took my suitcase to my room. As I passed by his office, the door was slightly ajar and Unchained Melody was quietly playing. I debated whether or not to tap on the door to let him know I was back, but for fear of getting yelled at, I decided to send him a text instead.

"I just wanted you to know that I'm back."

No response.

I went into Nora's room to check on her and found that she was sleeping. I didn't want to wake her, but I needed to check her vitals, so I did it as quietly as I could.

"Hey." She smiled as she slowly opened her eyes.

"Hi. I'm sorry I woke you."

"You didn't. I wasn't fully asleep anyway. Are you all packed for California?"

"I am." I grinned. "Tomorrow I'll help you get packed."

"Thanks."

"You're awake," Carter spoke as he walked into the room.

"Not for long." She softly smiled. "I'm really tired."

"Do you need anything before you go to sleep?" I asked.

"No. I'm fine," she whispered.

"Okay, get some rest." I patted her hand.

"Good night, Nora," Carter spoke as he walked over and kissed her head.

Just as we were walking out of the room, Nora called out Carter's name.

"Yes?" He turned around.

"Thank you."

He gave her a gentle smile and then went to the living room and poured himself a drink.

"Is this okay now?" His brow arched as he asked in a sarcastic tone.

"It's your house. Do whatever you want," I replied as I went into the kitchen.

I hadn't eaten dinner and I was hungry. Opening up the refrigerator, I pulled out some left over chicken casserole Sadie had made. After heating it up, I took a seat at the island and Carter walked in.

"That smells good."

"Would you like some?" I asked.

"Yeah. Actually, I think I will have some." He took the seat next to me.

I looked at him and wondered why he was sitting down instead of heating up his food. I continued to eat and caught him staring at me out of the corner of my eye.

"What?" I asked.

"Aren't you going to heat it up for me?"

"No. Why would I?"

"You asked if I wanted some."

"That didn't mean that I would heat it up for you." I cocked my head.

He sat there with a narrowed eye and slowly nodded his head.

"This is payback for the coffee, isn't it?"

"I have no clue what you're talking about."

He sighed, got up from the stool, and heated himself a plate. Inside, I was silently laughing because it *was* payback for the coffee incident.

****

Carter

I rented a private jet to fly us to California. When we arrived at our beach house, a sickness filled me. I slowly closed my eyes as I took in a deep breath. Our driver brought Nora's wheelchair up to the porch while I inserted the key and unlocked the door. Sadie and Zoey stepped inside while I went back to the car to get Nora. After setting her in her wheelchair, I stood in the foyer as all the memories came flooding back in my mind.

"This is beautiful," Zoey spoke.

"Welcome to Casa Grayson in Malibu." Nora smiled.

"I had one of the rooms down here made up for you," I spoke to Nora.

"Thanks, big brother. Hey, are you okay?" She lightly grabbed my hand.

"I'm fine."

"I want to go down to the beach," she spoke.

"Now?" I asked. "I think we should get settled first."

"I'll take her." Zoey smiled.

"Fine. Maybe I'll come down in a while," I spoke as I walked away.

I took my bags up to my bedroom, and I swallowed hard as my hand slowly turned the knob and I opened the door. I stood there, paralyzed, as I stared into the room.

"It's a beautiful day to spend on the beach." She smiled as her lips pressed against my chest.

"Is that what we're doing today?" I kissed the top of her head.

"Do you have a better idea?" she asked.

"I think I might." I rolled her on her back and hovered over her.

"Is that so?" She grinned.

"It is. But it's a surprise. So you'll have to wait."

"Not too long, I hope. Now you have me in suspense. I love surprises."

"And I love surprising you." My lips softly brushed against hers.

My eyes started to fill with tears, but I needed to remember why I was here.

Chapter Fourteen

Zoey

I left Nora in her wheelchair on the patio while I went upstairs to get Carter. I needed his help getting her down to the beach. When I reached the top of the stairs, I saw him standing in the doorway of what I presumed was his bedroom.

"Hey, are you okay?" I asked.

He turned and looked at me with a disapproving look and stepped inside the room.

"I'm fine. I thought you were taking Nora to the beach."

"About that. I need your help. I can't push the wheelchair in the sand and she's too weak to walk, even with my help."

"I'll be down in a minute," he spoke in an irritated tone.

"Yeah. Okay," I softly spoke and then went back downstairs.

A few moments later, Carter met us on the patio, picked up Nora from her wheelchair, and carried her down to where two chairs sat in the sand.

"When you're ready to come back up, call me," he spoke to her.

"Thank you, Carter." She placed her hand on his arm. "You don't want to stay with us?"

"No. I'm sorry."

As soon as he walked away, I stared straight ahead at the blue ocean water, taking in the sounds of the waves hitting the shoreline.

"I feel bad for making him come here, but he needed to," Nora spoke as she looked over at me.

"What do you mean? How long has it been?"

"Five years. He hasn't been back here since Angelique and the baby died."

"Why didn't he sell it then?" I asked out of curiosity.

"I wouldn't let him. The house is also in my name and I enjoy coming here. I know the memories are very painful for him, but he needs to face his pain and move on. He brought Angelique here to propose to her on this very beach just as the sun was setting. I'll never forget that night he called me and told me she said yes. He was so excited."

"I'm sure he was," I spoke.

"I need to ask you something and I want the truth from you, Zoey."

"Of course, Nora. What is it?"

"What did you mean when you told me you had a gift? That day you asked me about Angelique?"

I stared straight ahead at the ocean. A light breeze swept over my face before answering her question.

"I died when I was five years old, but it wasn't my time, so they sent me back. When I woke up, I had an ability. The ability to see people who have passed on."

"So you've been to Heaven?"

"I have, and it's the most beautiful and peaceful place." I rested my hand on hers. "You have nothing to fear, Nora. I promise you."

"I'm not afraid. Especially now that you're here. You mentioned to me before that Carter's energy is very dark. Is that also something you can see?"

"I can see people's auras and his is very black, which makes sense with the way he lives his life."

"He keeps his emotions and feelings tightly locked up inside him," she spoke. "He won't heal, Zoey, and now with what's happening to me, he'll be alone and that terrifies me. That is why I need your help."

"Like I told you before, I can only try and help him if he wants to be helped."

She gave my hand a gentle squeeze.

"If anyone can get through to him, you can. I know it. I can feel it."

I gave her a tender smile as the light breeze swept across my face.

"Are you ready to come back inside?" Carter asked as he walked up behind us.

"Yes. I need to lie down," Nora replied.

He picked her up from the chair, and carried her back to the house and into her bedroom. I followed behind and made sure she was comfortable.

"I've opened your window so you can hear the ocean," Carter spoke.

"Thank you. If the two of you don't mind, I'm going to go to sleep now."

Carter and I left the room and headed to the kitchen.

"I put your bags in the room next to Nora's," he spoke. "There's only four bedrooms, two downstairs and two upstairs. Sadie and I will be upstairs."

"Okay. Thanks," I spoke.

I walked over to the refrigerator and grabbed a bottle of water. Standing in front of the sink, I took a sip as I stared out the large window at the beautiful ocean view.

"It's beautiful here. I can see why you bought it," I spoke.

"Yeah, well, it will be going up for sale after—" He stopped.

I could feel his pain and anguish and I knew this house once held good memories for him, but he only saw them as bad ones. And as long as he stayed in this state, he would never live the life he was meant to live. I took in a deep breath.

"Memories are only bad because of the pain we let ourselves consume."

"Excuse me?" he spoke.

"Nothing." I shook my head.

"No! What did you mean by that?" He scowled as he approached me.

"I know how much it hurts you to be in this house and you're only here because it's Nora's dying wish. But it doesn't have to hurt, Mr. Grayson. Memories are a treasure and they were made with love. That's what you need to remember. Embrace the memories here. Feel the good times and the love and remember what it's like to live again."

Anger consumed his eyes as he stared deeply into mine. I wasn't turning away and I wasn't letting him win. He needed to hear the words I had just spoken. Even if it meant that he would hate me even more than he already did.

"You don't know what the fuck you're talking about!" He pointed his finger at me. "Stay out of my fucking business and my life!" he spoke through gritted teeth before turning his back and storming out the patio door.

I inhaled a deep breath and went to check on Nora.

****

Sadie made a nice dinner, and when I went into Nora's room to see if she was hungry, she slowly opened her eyes.

"Are you up to eating anything?" I asked as I walked over and placed my hand on hers.

"I just need some water," she moaned.

I picked up the cup of water from the nightstand and brought the straw up to her mouth. The moment she took a sip, she started choking.

"It's getting harder to swallow," she whispered as she lay back down. "I'm getting weaker and the headaches are getting worse. I've done all my research and I know what you have to do now. Prepare Carter for it, please." She looked at me as a tear fell from her eye.

"I will, but right now, I need to call the doctor. I'll be right back."

I walked out of her room and into mine. Grabbing the white piece of paper from my purse, I made a call to Doctor Sutton, who was the physician that Nora's doctor back in New York assigned to her while she was here in California. He was fully aware of her condition and prescribed everything she needed.

"Sadie made dinner for us and you can't be bothered to sit and eat it? I thought you were just checking on Nora," he spoke in a nasty tone as he stood in the doorway of my room.

"I need to talk to you, Mr. Grayson."

"You can talk to me at the dinner table." He scowled as he walked away.

Rolling my eyes, I stepped into Nora's room to check on her and she was sound asleep. Walking into the dining room, I took the seat across from Carter and placed the napkin in my lap.

"What do you need to discuss with me?" he asked.

"I made a call to Dr. Sutton and he will be stopping by in about an hour to examine Nora and bring some supplies for her."

"Why?"

"She's having trouble swallowing and her headaches are getting worse. She's going to need to be hooked up to an IV for fluids from here on out and it will be easier to push her meds when she needs them."

"How the fuck is she supposed to eat? Are you going to give her a feeding tube?"

"At this point, a feeding tube will only provide her with liquids her body no longer needs and that can cause her to swell, making her more uncomfortable."

"So you're going to let her starve to death? Is that what you're telling me?" he shouted.

"Mr. Grayson, her body no longer needs the nutrition and she has no appetite. You've witnessed how she's been eating the past couple of weeks. I'll have Sadie make her some cream of wheat if she wants food, but to be honest, she's not going to want anything. Now we just have to try and make her as comfortable as possible."

He threw his napkin on the table, got up from his chair, and stormed out the patio door. I stood up and watched as he walked down to the beach. Sadie looked at me as I went to go after him.

"Don't, Zoey. Let him be for a while. If you go out there now, you'll only make it worse. He needs time to process what you just told him."

"You're right." I sighed as I sat down, picked up my fork and began to eat.

Chapter Fifteen

Carter

I walked across the sand, shoes and socks still on my feet, and stood with my hands tucked in my pants pockets while I stared into the vast open water. Slowly closing my eyes, I listened to the crashing sounds of the waves as they hit the shoreline and the screams of the seagulls that flew overhead. As much as I thought I was prepared for this, I wasn't.

After a while, I went back up to the house.

"Where's Zoey?" I asked Sadie.

"She and the doctor are in with Nora," she replied with a sad look.

I walked over to Nora's bedroom and stood quietly at the door, watching the doctor examine her as Zoey hung the IV.

"You must be Mr. Grayson," the doctor spoke. "Nora is resting comfortably and Zoey will keep me updated. Do you have any questions? I know how hard this is."

"No." I lightly shook my head. "I don't have any questions."

He gave me a sympathetic smile as he placed his hand on my shoulder.

"The best thing you can do is not to let her see you fall apart. She's weak and you need to be her strength."

We walked out of the room and I escorted him to the front door. After he left, I poured myself a glass of scotch and took it out on the patio. Darkness was falling and the stars were starting to make their appearance for the night. I took a seat in the lounge chair and sipped on my drink.

"Excuse me, Mr. Grayson. Is there anything I can get for you before I retire for the night?" Sadie asked.

"Tell Zoey I need to see her."

A few moments later, I heard the patio door slide open.

"You wanted to see me?" Zoey's voice spoke from behind.

"Have a seat." I pointed to the lounge chair next to me. "Has Nora discussed any funeral arrangements with you?"

"No. She hasn't. Why?"

I let out a long sigh. "She's being very secretive about it and I want to know why."

"What do you mean?" she asked.

"I tried to talk to her about what her wishes were, and she told me that she already has everything arranged, and I will find out the details after her death. Are you sure you don't know anything about it?"

"I'm positive, Mr. Grayson. She never said a word to me about it."

"How much longer does she have to suffer?"

"Possibly a week, maybe two."

"I need another drink," I spoke as I got up from my chair and walked into the house.

"Drinking isn't going to make all of this go away," Zoey spoke as she followed me inside.

"We're done talking, Zoey. I asked you a question, I got my answer, and now we're done."

I poured myself another scotch and brought the glass up to my lips. I stopped, set the glass down, and placed my hands on the bar. I needed to be sober for Nora.

****

One Week Later

In the course of a few days, Nora had multiple seizures, and every day, it was getting harder to watch her deteriorate. She was in and out of consciousness and pumped full of pain medication. I spent most of the day working in my office and holding meetings over Skype. Then I would go into her room, sit beside her bed, and talk to her. Half the time, she couldn't hear me, but it didn't matter.

I was sitting in my office when Zoey lightly knocked on the door.

"What is it?"

"Nora is asking for you," she spoke.

I could tell something was wrong because of the sadness in her voice. Getting up from my chair and with a sick feeling in my stomach, I went and sat beside Nora.

"Hey." I smiled. "I'm here now."

She looked at me and a weak smile framed her lips.

"You're going to be okay, Carter. Promise me."

Tears filled my eyes, and even though I would never be okay again, I couldn't tell her that.

"I'll be fine." I softly stroked her forehead. "I don't want you worrying about me."

"Growing up, you always worried about me. So now, it's my turn to worry about you. You're my brother and I love you," she spoke in a soft and weak tone.

"I love you too, Nora." I kissed her forehead.

"Zoey?" she called out.

"I'm right here," Zoey spoke as she walked over to her bedside and took hold of her hand.

"They're here. I can see them. Can you?"

Zoey smiled as she softly spoke, "Yes. I can see them."

Nora turned her head and stared out the window as she took her last breath. Tears started to stream down my face as I lowered my head on her chest.

Chapter Sixteen

Zoey

You would think when my patients died, it would be the hardest part of my job. But it wasn't. Nora's battle with her illness had ended and she was no longer suffering. Her soul left her body and she joined hands with her mother and father, who were waiting to take her home. Before fading into the distance, she turned to me and smiled. I smiled back as I waved goodbye to her.

I decided to leave the room and give Carter some time alone with his sister. Walking into my bedroom, I took my phone from the nightstand and called Dr. Sutton to let him know Nora had passed. Then, per Nora's instructions upon her death, I called her attorney.

"Who were you talking to?" Carter asked as he stood in the doorway of my room.

"I had to call Dr. Sutton and Nora's attorney."

"Why her attorney?" he asked.

"I don't know. Nora gave me specific instructions to call him immediately after she—" I looked down. "Someone will be here soon to take her body, so if you need some more time…"

"I'm fine. Sadie is in there now. I have no fucking clue what I'm supposed to do. She told me that everything for her funeral was taken care of and I didn't have to worry about a thing. So now what? How the fuck do I know what to do?"

"All I know is her attorney is on the next flight out of New York. He'll be here tonight. I'm sure she made all the arrangements with him."

"This doesn't make any sense to me. Why wouldn't she tell me and let me handle it?"

"I have no clue, Mr. Grayson. I wish I had some answers for you, but she never discussed her arrangements with me. So, we'll have to wait until he gets here."

He shook his head and walked away. My job here was over, at least with taking care of Nora. She wanted me to try and help Carter through it, but I didn't know how I was going to. The minute we got back to New York, we'd part ways, and I'd probably never see him again. Not by any choice of mine, but his. I was sure he couldn't wait to get rid of me. I went into Nora's room, expecting to find Carter in there, but he wasn't.

"Have you seen Mr. Grayson, Sadie?" I asked.

"No. I haven't," she spoke with sadness as her teary eyes looked at me.

I walked around the house to see where he had gone, and I couldn't find him. I even went up to his room, but he wasn't there. Walking into the kitchen, I decided to make a pot of coffee. While I waited for it to brew, I placed my hands on the kitchen counter and stared out the window. That was when I saw Carter standing on the beach, facing the water.

I was startled by a knock on the door, and when I opened it, two tall gentlemen stood there with their hands clasped in front of them.

"Can I help you?"

"We're from Kingsley Funeral Home and we're here to collect the body of Nora Grayson."

"Please, come in."

I led them to Nora's room and let them do their job while I went down to the beach to get Carter.

"Excuse me, Mr. Grayson?"

He turned and looked at me.

"The funeral home is here to pick up Nora. I thought you should know."

"What funeral home?" he asked.

"Kingsley," I replied.

He hastily walked back to the house and into Nora's room.

"Excuse me, but who called you to pick up my sister's body?"

"A man named Mr. Gainsley."

"And what are you going to do with her body? She needs to be flown back to New York."

"I'm sorry, but I don't know. The only thing we were told was that we needed to pick up the body and further instructions will be given to us tomorrow."

"Damn it." He shook his head.

I walked over to him and lightly took hold of his arm. I knew I was crossing the line, but I didn't care. He wasn't going to make a scene.

"Mr. Grayson, let's go into the kitchen and let them do their job. I've made some coffee."

He looked down at my hand on his arm and then up at me.

"Coffee? You really think I want fucking coffee right now?" he angrily spoke as he left the room.

I followed him down the hallway and into the living room, where he picked up a bottle of scotch and poured himself a glass.

"This is what I want." He held up his glass. "Not a fucking cup of coffee."

I bit my tongue because he was lashing out from anger and hurt over Nora's death. If the only way he could cope right now was to drink, then so be it. I turned away and walked into the kitchen where Sadie had started preparing dinner.

"You don't need to do that, Sadie."

"I do, Zoey. I need to keep busy."

The men from the funeral home carried Nora's body out and had Carter sign some papers.

"Let me ask you something," Carter spoke as he approached me. "What did Nora mean when she said 'they' were here? Who did she see?"

I didn't want to tell him because I knew he wouldn't be able to handle it. So I hesitated.

"I asked you a question and I expect an answer," he spoke in an angry tone.

"Your parents."

He let out a loud, roaring laugh.

"And you expect me to believe that? She was delirious."

"I don't expect you to believe anything, Mr. Grayson. You asked me a question and I answered it."

"You're fucking nuts." He pointed at me. "You may take good care of dying patients, but you're not right in the head."

He grabbed the bottle of scotch and took it upstairs.

"Don't listen to him, Zoey. He isn't aware of what he's saying," Sadie spoke.

"I know he doesn't." I sighed.

I ate dinner with Sadie, helped her clean up, and headed to my room for the night. When I stepped out of the shower, my phone rang. It was Mr. Gainsley.

"Hello," I answered.

"Miss Benson, it's Brian Gainsley. I just landed and I'm going to get a hotel room for the night. I'll be by tomorrow say around ten?"

"Ten o'clock will be fine, Mr. Gainsley."

"See you then," he spoke.

Before climbing into bed, I decided to check on Carter. The door to his bedroom was slightly opened, and when I took a peek inside, I noticed he wasn't in there. Opening the door all the way, I looked around and saw nothing. So I went downstairs and noticed the patio door wasn't slid shut all the way. I went back to my room, put on a pair of sweatpants and a tank top, and went down to the beach.

"Mr. Grayson." I knelt down beside him as he lay on his back in the sand with the empty scotch bottle lying beside him.

He let out a moan and tried to roll over. I sighed and shook my head as I grabbed his arm and tried to get him up.

"Come on, Carter, you have to help me out here."

Another moan escaped his lips.

"As much as I want to leave your dumb drunk ass out here all night, Nora would never forgive me. So come on!" I shouted.

I managed to sit him up and he looked at me.

"I can't believe she's gone," he slurred.

"I know. We can talk about this later, after you've sobered up."

I helped him up, hooked his arm around my neck, and practically dragged him back to the house. There was no way he was getting up the stairs, so I led him over to the couch and helped him lie down. I ran up to his room and grabbed his pillow from the bed and a white blanket that sat on a chair. After covering him and making sure he was comfortable, I went to bed.

Chapter Seventeen

Carter

I was awoken out of a sound sleep by the feeling of being poked. Slowly opening my eyes, I saw Zoey standing over me.

"What the fuck are you doing?" I mumbled as I placed my arm over my head.

"Nora's attorney will be here in an hour and you reek like alcohol. Get yourself up, get in the shower, and get dressed. I brought you some coffee."

"Why didn't you wake me up sooner?" I asked.

"I tried. You wouldn't wake up."

I managed to sit myself up and take the coffee cup from her hands.

"Why am I on the couch? I thought I was in bed."

"I found you passed out on the beach last night and I could only manage to drag you this far. You're lucky I didn't leave you out there all night."

"You didn't have to do that." I brought the cup up to my lips.

"I know I didn't have to, but I wasn't going to let you embarrass yourself."

I closed my eyes to try and soothe the massive headache that consumed me.

"I better go shower before he gets here."

I got up from the couch and slowly walked up the stairs. Standing under the hot water and letting it stream down my body, I thought about all the changes my life was going to have now that Nora was gone. I hated change. I used to welcome it because I believed at one time it was good for the soul, but these changes I'd experienced over the past years were nothing but fucking torture. I was a thirty-year-old man who had more money than I knew what do with and it didn't matter. If I could give it all up to have my loved ones back, I would in a heartbeat. The more I thought about it, the angrier I became.

After I finished showering and getting dressed, I headed downstairs and heard a knock at the door. Walking over to it, I turned the knob and saw Brian Gainsley standing there.

"Hello, Carter. I'm so sorry for your loss."

"Thanks, Brian. Come on in."

"You must be Miss Benson." He smiled as he held out his hand.

"It's Zoey. Nice to meet you, Mr. Gainsley."

"I suppose we should go into the dining room," I spoke. "May I get you anything, Brian? Coffee? A drink perhaps?"

"No thank you." He took a seat at the table.

Zoey took her seat and I sat down next to her.

"I have Nora's wishes, so to speak. I was instructed to deliver these wishes immediately following her death."

He pulled out a large packet of papers from the envelope and cleared his throat.

"I, Nora Grayson, give to you the following that are my wishes and are to be honored upon my death. I will be cremated and my ashes will be scattered in the following places: Lake Tahoe, Grand Canyon, in the waters of Puget Sound, and my remaining ashes shall be scattered near Sweetheart Rock on the Hawaiian Island of Lanai. The scattering is to be done by two people: my brother Carter Grayson and my hospice nurse Zoey Benson in the exact order as stated above."

"What?!" I exclaimed. "You have got to be kidding me."

"Shall I continue, Carter?" Brian asked with a raised brow.

I sat there and looked out the window as he continued.

"Upon the completion of my wishes, Zoey will receive a check for services rendered and Carter will receive the signed papers handing over my shares of Grayson Enterprises to him. Both Carter and Zoey will travel by car to distribute my ashes with the exception of Hawaii. Since Lanai will be the last place visited and not many ashes will be left, the remaining amount can be stored in a small Ziploc baggie and tucked away in between layers of clothing either in a carry-on or suitcase. Take note that when you scatter my ashes in Lake Tahoe, it must be done on the south side (Nevada), since it is prohibited in California. When you get back home to New York, please have a celebration lunch or dinner for me. Celebrate the fact that I am healthy once again and no longer in pain. No tears shall be shed and life will go on as usual."

"Well, that's it. Those are Nora's wishes," Brian spoke. "I've already been in contact with the funeral home and they will be cremating her today and you may pick up her ashes tomorrow. She was very prepared for this, Carter. Now it's up to you and Miss Benson to see that her wishes are fulfilled."

"She certainly was prepared, wasn't she?" I sighed.

"If you don't have any further questions, I have a plane to catch back to New York."

"No." I shook my head. "No questions."

"Again, I'm so sorry for your loss. She was a wonderful girl."

I walked Brian to the door, and after I shut it, I looked over at Zoey, who was still sitting at the table.

"What the hell was she thinking?" I asked.

"I don't know."

"Listen," I spoke as I walked over to her. "I can do this alone. I'll write you a check and you can go home."

"To be honest with you, Mr. Grayson, the last thing I want to do is to be stuck in a car with you traveling from state to state, but I respected Nora a great deal, and if this is what she wanted, then I will do as she asked."

I narrowed my eye at her at the fact that she said she didn't want to be stuck in a car with me.

"Fine. Then we'll head to Lake Tahoe tomorrow after we leave the funeral home."

"In what?" she asked.

"I guess I'll have to rent us a car, won't I?"

I left the dining room and headed down to the beach to do some thinking and call the rental car company. Me and Zoey, in a car for all those days and hours, alone. We barely got along as it was, and now, I had a feeling things were about to get worse. I was looking forward to parting ways with her in the next day or two. But now, we'd be stuck on this road trip together, which was already stressing me out and making my head hurt.

Chapter Eighteen

Zoey

The thought of being stuck in a car with him traveling through different states made me uncomfortable. I knew what Nora was thinking when she did that. The last thing she whispered to me before she passed was to look after him and make sure he was okay. If he had been a nice person, I wouldn't have minded. And even though he was rude, arrogant, and a total asshole of a human being, I still felt this undeniable pull towards him. Nora wasn't the only one who wanted me to help him. Angelique visited my dreams frequently. Her presence in this house was strong and her messages were coming through loud and clear.

"I've rented a car for our little road trip," Carter spoke from behind and I jumped.

"You scared me." I placed my hand over my heart and turned around. "Why are you always sneaking up on me?"

"I don't sneak up on you. It's not my fault that you're always in a daze."

"I am not."

"Yes, you are. But I'm not going to stand here and argue with you. Sadie's flight back to New York leaves tomorrow morning at ten o'clock and the car service is picking her up at eight. As soon as she leaves, we'll head to the funeral home and be on our way to Lake Tahoe."

Just as I was about to speak, Carter's phone rang.

"I have to take this." He headed towards his office.

I went into the kitchen where Sadie was just starting to make lunch. As I was helping her, Carter walked in.

"As of tomorrow, this house will be on the market."

"That was quick," I spoke.

"The quicker the better."

He walked over to the refrigerator and grabbed a bottle of water.

"But why? You bought this house for a reason at one time."

Sadie glanced over at me and lightly shook her head as if to warn me not to agitate him, but I didn't care. Carter turned to me, his eyes burned into mine.

"Me selling this house is none of your concern, Zoey."

"You're right, Mr. Grayson, it's not. But this house meant the world to Nora. She wouldn't want you to sell it."

"Nora isn't here anymore, is she?" He cocked his head and spoke with an attitude.

"Just because she isn't physically here doesn't mean she isn't here in spirit."

"Jesus Christ, enough with your craziness. Nora isn't here, this is my house, and I've decided to sell it. There's no need for me to keep it anymore."

"The memories here are enough to want to keep it," I spoke.

"Yeah, well, some memories are better forgotten. I'm going out. I'll be back later." He stormed out of the kitchen.

I looked at Sadie, who stood there with an "I told you so" look on her face. I shrugged.

"Someone had to say it. He's selling this house for all the wrong reasons and one day he will regret it."

"*We* know that, Zoey, but he will never see it that way."

I was lying in bed, unable to fall asleep, when I heard the front door open. Looking at the clock, I saw that it was just after midnight. I listened carefully for him to walk up the stairs, but I didn't hear anything. It wasn't hard to miss because the third step from the bottom squeaked when you stepped on it. Was he drunk again? Did he need to be checked on? Why did I care? I lay there, pondering my thoughts, and finally threw the covers back and walked from my room to the living area, where I found Carter lying on the couch, passed out. Walking back to my room, I grabbed an extra pillow off the bed and a blanket, and took it out to him. After placing the pillow under his head and covering him with the blanket, I stood there for a moment and stared at him. His grief, his broken heart, and his broken soul were too much for him to handle and I wasn't sure how to help him.

****

The next morning, after getting dressed, I grabbed my bags and set them by the front door. Looking over at the couch, I noticed Carter wasn't there. As I went into the kitchen for a cup of coffee, I heard footsteps coming down the stairs.

"Sadie will be down in a minute. Are you all packed?" he spoke.

"Good morning to you too. My bags are already by the front door."

I poured him a cup of coffee and handed it to him.

"Were you the one responsible for the pillow and blanket last night?"

"Yes." I wrapped my hands around the mug and took a sip of coffee.

He stood in front of the patio door and stared out at the ocean.

"Thanks," he softly spoke.

"You're welcome. Want to talk about it?" I cautiously asked, even though I knew what the answer would be.

"No," he spoke in a sharp tone.

Sadie walked down the stairs just as there was a knock at the door.

"That must be your driver," Carter spoke to her.

I walked over and hugged her tight.

"Thank you for everything, Sadie."

"You're welcome, Zoey. Thank you for everything you did for Nora. Please don't be a stranger and come visit. I'll miss you and our morning talks."

I gave her a small smile.

"I'll miss you too, and I won't be a stranger."

"Good luck on your road trip. Whatever you do, please don't kill Mr. Grayson," she whispered to me with a smile.

"I will try my best to control myself." I winked at her.

Carter said his goodbyes, and as soon as Sadie was gone, he grabbed his bags.

"Are you ready?" he asked me.

"Is the rental car here?"

"Yes. It was dropped off last night."

Walking over to the door, I grabbed my bags and took them outside. While Carter loaded them into the Escalade he rented, I stood in front of the house and took one last look at it. Staring up at the bedroom window that was Carter's, I saw Angelique in the window. The corners of my mouth curved up into a tender smile as I climbed into the SUV and braced myself for the journey that I was about to embark on.

Carter drove us to the funeral home, which was only fifteen minutes down the road. Once we arrived, we were greeted by Ted Kingsley, the owner.

"I'm so sorry for your loss. Please step into my office and I will collect your sister's ashes," he spoke.

Carter and I took a seat in the oversized brown leather chairs and waited for Ted to come back. As I glanced over at him, I could see his uneasiness as he sat there and rubbed his hands. A few moments later, Ted and another man walked in carrying two small silver urns each.

"Why are there four urns?" Carter asked.

"It was per your sister's request," Ted replied. "Each urn is for the four places in which you will scatter her ashes."

He set the urns on the table next to his desk.

"Each urn is equally filled except for this one. This has only a small amount of her ashes in it for your Hawaii trip, which can easily be transferred into this plastic storage bag."

"I am not putting my sister's ashes in a plastic storage bag," Carter spoke. "I will be renting a private plane to fly us to Hawaii, so taking the urn won't be an issue."

"Very well, Mr. Grayson. All I need from you is a signature that you've picked up your sister's ashes and then we'll be done here."

Carter signed the paperwork, handed me two of the urns, and then we climbed into the SUV and started on our trip to Lake Tahoe.

Chapter Nineteen

Carter

I'd never had to pick up someone's ashes before. My parents and Angelique were buried in a coffin in the ground with gravestones for people to visit them. I wouldn't have that with Nora, and in a way, it pissed me off more than I ever knew it would. I took in a deep breath as I started the SUV and pulled out of the parking lot of the funeral home.

"I can't believe Nora did all this," I spoke in a hasty tone.

"Did what? Make things easy for you?"

I glanced over at Zoey, who was staring at me through her sunglasses.

"You think this is easy? You think I like traveling around with my sister's ashes in the back seat? I don't know why the hell she just couldn't be buried next to my parents."

"She obviously had a reason for wanting her ashes scattered to these various places. They must have some sort of meaning."

"If they do, I don't know anything about it."

"So do you have a plan or are we just winging it?" she asked.

"Like I had time to plan anything," I replied. "I guess we're just winging it. Can you do me a favor and just be quiet? I need to think."

"Maybe you should have started planning yesterday after Mr. Gainsley left instead of going out and getting drunk."

"Are you serious right now?" I glared at her. "What I do is none of your fucking business. Got it?" I pointed my finger at her.

"Got it, Mr. Grayson." She put in her earbuds and stared out the passenger side window.

Who the hell did she think she was?

The next two hours were quiet ones. Zoey listened to her music while I drove down the highway and thought about things. The things I had to do once I got back to New York. I glanced over at Zoey from time to time. I knew how rude I was being, but I couldn't help it. She was beautiful and she didn't deserve to be treated the way I treated her since the first day we met. But I couldn't let any type of feelings emerge. The man I used to be was gone, buried alive beneath the tragedies and pain I'd endured over the past few years. I was lost and Zoey seemed to be the type of woman who could find me. If I wanted to be found, I would let her. But I didn't. Because if I was, then I'd be forced to live a life of happiness, only to have it stolen away from me at any given time.

"Hey," I spoke as I looked over at Zoey.

She couldn't hear me, so I tapped on her shoulder. Taking her earbuds out, she spoke, "What?"

"Are you getting hungry?" I asked.

"Yeah. Actually, I am."

"In another hour, we'll be in Lone Pine, which is halfway to Lake Tahoe. We can stop and grab some lunch. Can you hold out?"

"I can." She smiled as she placed her earbuds back in her ears.

Her smile was her best feature as far as I was concerned. It was genuinely sweet and each time the corners of her mouth curved upwards, it sent an unexpected warmth through me. A warmth that I had to fight off every time. We reached Lone Pine and stopped at a restaurant called The Grill. The moment we stepped inside, Zoey ran to the bathroom while the hostess sat us in a booth near the window.

"Whew, I didn't think I was going to make it," she spoke as she sat down.

"Why didn't you say something? We could have stopped."

"You told me to be quiet so you could think," she replied.

I sighed as I picked up the menu.

"Listen, Zoey. We're going to be spending a lot of time together during this trip, so I think it would be in both our best interests if we tried to get along."

"I'm not the one with the problem, Mr. Grayson." Her brow raised.

"For fuck sakes. Can you please just stop with your comments? I'm trying really hard here to be nice."

"Then you're going to have to try a little harder."

I clenched my jaw, and before I could say anything, the waitress came to our table to take our order.

"What can I get you folks?" she asked.

"I'll have the cobb salad with honey mustard dressing, please," Zoey spoke.

"And for you, sir?"

"I'll have the turkey club with fries."

"Okie dokie. I'll put that in for you."

I stared at Zoey from across the table. I was going to say something in response to her last comment, but I decided not to. She didn't know what the hell she was talking about.

"We should be getting to Lake Tahoe around six o'clock. We'll find a hotel, grab some dinner, and scatter Nora's ashes tomorrow morning. Then we'll get on the road and head to the Grand Canyon, which is about a twelve-hour drive."

"Okay."

"I'm thinking about renting a private jet to fly us from the Grand Canyon to Seattle because it's almost a nineteen-hour drive."

"Nora specifically stated that we were to drive to these places except for Hawaii."

"Do you really want to be stuck in a car for nineteen hours?" I asked.

"It doesn't bother me. I'm sure it's a beautiful drive. And again, Nora said no planes except to Hawaii."

"Nora isn't here anymore and she won't know. The only thing that matters is that we scatter her ashes."

"Trust me, she'll know." Her brow raised.

I sighed.

"Don't start with that again, Zoey. Please. I'm in no mood."

The waitress came with our food and set the plates down in front of us. Our lunch consisted of nothing but good food and silence. Regardless of what Zoey thought, I was renting a private jet to fly us to Seattle.

Chapter Twenty

Zoey

After we finished our lunch, we climbed into the SUV and got back on the road to Lake Tahoe. Carter pulled his phone from his pocket and contacted several private jet agencies that were unable to accommodate his request from the Grand Canyon to Seattle. But he did manage to rent a plane to get us to Hawaii.

"This is bullshit," he shouted as he threw his phone down. "How can there not be one fucking plane available?"

I was silently smiling inside because I knew why. Nora didn't want us flying to Seattle and she made sure it didn't happen.

"The minute I get back to New York, I'm buying my own fucking plane."

I sat there in silence and let him rant and rave.

"Aren't you going to say anything?" he asked as he glanced over at me with his aviator sunglasses on.

"I'm sorry you couldn't get a plane and I'm sorry you have to be stuck with me on this road trip. Once we scatter Nora's ashes and get back to New York, you will never have to see me again, Mr. Grayson."

He glanced over at me and didn't say a word. Several moments passed, and suddenly, he pulled off to the side of the expressway.

"What are you doing?" I asked.

"Before we go any further, I think we need to have a talk. I don't feel like I'm stuck with you, so get that out of your head. I'm just frustrated. That's all. It has nothing to do with you and I don't want you to think that I don't want you on this trip. I've been through a lot, Zoey, and now that I've lost my sister, it just makes life a hell of a lot worse. You were there for Nora and I appreciate it. It just makes me mad that this is what she wanted and chose not to discuss any of it with me before she died. I visit the cemetery every Sunday, and now she won't be there for me to visit her."

This was the first time since I'd met him that he opened up to me and I was grateful for it. I reached over and placed my hand on top of his. I didn't care if he wanted me to do it or not, he needed comforting.

"Cemeteries are good places, Mr. Grayson, but you need to understand that your loved ones are around you at all times. It's only their bodies that are underground and that's why people think they need to visit cemeteries. They do it out of respect for their loved ones, but their spirits/souls are around you at all times. You can talk to Nora anytime you want and she'll hear you."

"I don't believe in any of that. I'm sorry." He removed his hand from under mine.

"It's okay. I can't make you believe anything you don't want to. But Nora can hear you wherever you are."

He took in a deep breath and pulled back onto the highway.

"Can you do me a favor and look up some hotels in Lake Tahoe?" he asked.

"Sure." I gave him a small smile as I pulled out my phone and noticed I had a text message from Holly.

"Hey, how's the road trip going?"

"Not good. He's still the same old Carter Grayson. Mean, arrogant, and filled with anger. So far, I can't seem to get through to him about anything."

"You will eventually. Just hang in there."

"Thanks, Holly."

"Text me some pictures later when you get to Lake Tahoe."

"I will."

I pulled up local hotels around Lake Tahoe.

"Is there a specific hotel you're looking for?" I asked him.

"Something that's a five star."

"There's a Hyatt Regency Resort, Spa, and Casino that's a five star."

I read the description to him and he told me to call and book two rooms.

"They only have a one bedroom cottage available for tonight," I spoke.

"Of course that's all they have," he spoke in a harsh tone. "Just hang up and call another hotel."

I called the other three that were five-star hotels and all of them were fully booked.

"Now what do you want me to do?" I asked.

"I guess we have no choice. Dial the other hotel and hand me your phone," he spoke in an irritated manner.

After reserving the only room available, he handed me my phone back.

"Is this the type of problem we're going to run into this whole goddamn trip?" he angrily spoke.

"I think the best thing to do when we get to Lake Tahoe, is we should look up hotels for all the other places and book them tonight."

"We're going to have to. Especially in Hawaii. We'll be lucky if we don't have to sleep on the beach," he spoke.

"Well, hopefully, it won't come to that. But I'm not sure sleeping on a blanket in the sand with the roaring sound of the waves and the smell of the ocean would be so bad." I softly smiled.

He looked over at me, and when he saw the smile on my face, the corners of his mouth slightly curved upwards.

****

Carter

The moment she placed her hand on mine, I felt like I was going to jump out of my skin. A bolt of—fuck if I knew—jolted through me. There was only one other time in my life when I ever felt that. I remembered the feeling and I remembered it was many years ago, but I couldn't remember when or where. Sharing a one-bedroom cottage with her was going to be difficult. But it was only for one night, and as soon as we got to Lake Tahoe, I would immediately book other hotels we needed during the course of our trip.

"I need to pull off and get gas. You should try to use the restroom while we're there," I spoke.

"Good idea." She smiled.

At the next exit, I got off and pulled into the first gas station I saw. I got out of the car and started to pump gas while Zoey went to the bathroom. As I stood there, holding the pump, I looked around, taking in the sight of the mountains. When I was finished, I couldn't believe Zoey wasn't back yet, so I went inside the station to look for her.

"Are you hungry?" I asked as I found her in the candy aisle.

"Just having a little sweet tooth at the moment." She grinned.

"Pick out anything you want. It's on me. In fact, I think I'll grab a couple things myself."

We both reached at the same time for the Snickers bar and our fingers lightly touched.

"You like Snickers?" I asked as I looked at her.

"I do. I guess you do too."

"It's one of my favorites."

"Mine too." She smiled.

I grabbed the candy bar from the box and handed it to her. She graciously accepted and picked up a box of Junior Mints.

"These used to be my mom's—" She suddenly stopped and began to walk away.

A feeling sank inside me. She told me that she was abandoned as a baby on the stairs of a church. In fact, her father, John, told me the same thing. What the hell was going on?

"How could you possibly remember what your mom's favorite candy was if you never knew your mother?" I asked.

She swallowed hard and walked up to the cash register.

"Zoey, answer me."

"Sometimes I call my dad Scott 'Mom.' It was hard growing up with two fathers and no mother. Sometimes, the kids at school made fun of me."

She was lying. I could feel it. But I was going to let it go for now. Soon enough I'd find out the truth.

"I see. I'm sure that was hard," I spoke.

I pulled my wallet from my pocket and handed the cashier some cash.

"Are you ready?" I asked her as I grabbed the bag from the counter.

Chapter Twenty-One

Zoey

I let out a breath. He seemed to believe me. But there was one thing that Carter Grayson wasn't, and that was stupid. I could trust him to tell him about my past, but he wasn't ready to hear it, so it was best to keep my mouth shut, at least for now.

Carter pulled up to the valet at the Hyatt Regency Resort & Spa. A nice young gentleman wearing square-rimmed glasses took our bags from the car and set them on the ground. Grabbing mine, I headed through the double doors that were being held open by another nice young man with a genuine smile.

"Good day, Miss." He tipped his hat.

"Good day." I smiled.

Carter said hello and I followed him up to the reservations desk.

"How may I help you, sir?" The cute brunette behind the desk smiled brightly.

"Reservation for Carter Grayson."

"I'll just need your driver's license and credit card." She grinned. "I see you've rented our one-bedroom cottage."

"Like I had a choice," he spoke with a slight attitude. "It's the only thing you had available."

"I'm sorry about that, Mr. Grayson. It's one of our busiest times of the year. But I can promise you that you'll love it. Our cottages are so cozy and the view of the lake is amazing. Plus, you're only a couple of steps away from the beach."

"As nice as that sounds, it's only a one-bedroom."

The cute brunette looked over at me in confusion.

"We aren't dating or anything. In fact, I don't even think we're friends, so he's uncomfortable with the fact that there's only one bed," I spoke.

Carter glanced at me with furrowed brows.

"Oh," the cute brunette spoke. "The couch is very comfortable."

"Just give us the keys, please," Carter spoke to her.

"Of course, Mr. Grayson. I'll have Miguel, our bellhop, take your bags and show you the way. Your cottage is on the lower level, so it does feature a half bath as well."

"Wow. It sounds better already," he spoke in a sarcastic tone.

As soon as she handed him the keys, Carter walked away without as so much as a thank you.

"I'm so sorry," I spoke to her. "His sister just passed away and he's having a hard time."

"I understand. I hope you enjoy your stay."

"I know I will. Him, I'm not so sure." I gave her a small smile and followed him and Miguel, the bellhop, to cottage number three.

As soon as we stepped inside the cottage, Miguel set our bags down and Carter handed him a tip.

"This is so cute." I smiled as I looked around.

"If you say so," Carter spoke in a rude manner. "Why did you say all that to the girl at the desk?"

"Because she needed to know why you were being so rude. It's not her fault they only had this one-bedroom cottage available. In fact, you should be thankful that we even got this. Anyway, I will take the couch tonight."

"No. I'll take the couch. You can have the bed. What kind of man would I be making a woman sleep on the couch?"

The pain that radiated through my body as I bit down hard on my tongue jolted through me. Oh, the things I could have said to him. But I didn't.

"You paid for the room, Carter. It's only right I take the couch and you take the bed."

"This discussion is over. Understand? I'm taking the couch."

"Suit yourself." I put my hands up. "Wow, look at this view." I smiled as I walked over to the window.

Carter followed and stood next to me with his hands tucked into his pants pockets.

"It's nice. I can see why Nora wanted some of her ashes scattered here. Are you hungry? We can head to dinner."

"That sounds good."

We went up to the Lone Eagle Grill where Carter ordered the filet and I ordered the roasted chicken. Before our food was even ready, he had already downed two scotches compared to my one glass of wine.

"They have a casino downstairs. How about we go check it out after dinner?"

"I would like that, but how about you call some hotels and make reservations." I smirked.

"Shit. I didn't do that yet, did I?" He pulled his phone from his pocket and began searching hotels. "We can stay inside the park at one of these horrific hotels or stay in Sedona at a nice hotel and then drive a hundred miles to the Grand Canyon."

"That's about an hour and a half," I spoke.

"I really don't want to drive another hour and a half, scatter her ashes, and then drive nineteen hours to Seattle. Fuck!"

"I'll drive to the Grand Canyon," I spoke.

He glanced up from his phone and shot me a look of disapproval. The waitress came over and set our plates down in front of us.

"Enjoy your dinner." She smiled. "May I get you another drink, sir?"

"Yes, please," Carter spoke.

"If we scatter Nora's ashes here tomorrow morning around eight, we can be on the road by nine," I spoke.

"What's your point, Zoey?"

"By time we get to the Grand Canyon, it'll be at least nine p.m. and we'll both be exhausted, so we won't have time to think about how crappy the hotel is because we'll go right to bed."

"Crappy hotels equal crappy, uncomfortable beds. If I'm driving twelve hours, then I want to make sure the bed is comfortable."

"Okay. Then book a hotel in Sedona and stop complaining," I spewed as I took a bite of my chicken.

"Fine. I will." He glared at me.

"In fact, maybe we should just stay two nights."

"What? Why the hell would we do that?" His brow arched.

"Because you're already going to be tired from driving twelve hours, and then you're going to drive another nineteen or even twenty the next day? I know that I'll need a break from the car, at least for a day. I think if we're stuck together in the car all that time, we'll end up killing each other." I smirked.

"No. We're only staying one night." He took a bite of his filet. "And as for the possibility of killing each other, we'll make some stops along the way and give each other a break."

"Okay. If you say so. But, it's going to take us a lot longer to get to Seattle."

After calling a few hotels with no luck, Carter finally was able to book a two-bedroom suite at the Enchantment Resort in Sedona.

"Thank God," he sighed.

"I like the name." I smiled. "It sounds like a fairytale place."

"I'll only consider it a fairytale place if the bed is comfortable. Which, for the price it's costing me for one night, it better be."

I gave him a small smile and finished my dinner. Before paying the bill, Carter had one more scotch.

"I think we should head back to the cottage," he spoke. "Forget the casino."

"Good idea. I'm exhausted anyway."

When we got back to the cottage, Carter let me use the bathroom first to get ready for bed since the half bath light was burnt out. After changing into my nightshirt, I grabbed a blanket from the closet and a pillow and took it to the couch.

"What are you doing?" he asked.

"I've decided that I'm taking the couch and I don't want to hear a word about it. You drove all day and we have a very long drive tomorrow. So I want you to get a good night's sleep."

"I don't give a damn what you want, Zoey. I'm taking the couch. I thought we had an understanding."

"*You* thought we had an understanding, Mr. Grayson. I'm taking the couch. End of discussion."

He took a few steps closer to me and grabbed hold of the blanket in my hand. I pulled back and before I knew it, we were playing tug of war.

"I'm taking the couch, Zoey." He pulled harder. "And don't take that tone with me."

"No, you're not, and I will take any tone I please. From now on, I will treat you with the same respect you treat me!"

He stopped pulling the blanket and his eyes burned into mine. He reached over and softly brushed his thumb over my lips. Shivers ran down my spine and my lips started to tremble. I swallowed hard, for I knew what was to come next. He leaned in and lightly pressed his mouth to mine. Our lips intertwined, and suddenly, everything bad about him seemed to have disappeared. Our kiss deepened and our tongues danced in excitement. A subtle moan escaped him as his hands slightly pushed up my nightshirt and planted themselves firmly on my ass, giving it a gentle squeeze.

"I need sex, Zoey," he whispered as he broke our kiss. "I need it desperately."

"Okay," I softly spoke.

"It means absolutely nothing. I need you to understand that."

"I do."

His mouth smashed into mine as he picked me up, carried me to the bedroom, and then set me down in front of the bed.

Chapter Twenty-Two

Carter

Seeing her in that red nightshirt with her hard nipples poking through the fabric sent me over the edge of sexual frustration. I needed to bury my cock inside her because I knew she could give me the stress relief and pleasure I needed.

I stood in front of her as my fingers gripped the bottom of her nightshirt and I slowly pulled it over her head. Instantly, my cock stood tall, rock hard in a matter of seconds. I didn't even need to touch her. Her perfect petite body and beauty was all I needed. She stood in front of me, her hourglass figure, perfect perky breasts, toned abdomen, and satin pink panties. I wrapped one hand around the nape of her neck as I softly kissed her lips, while my other hand went straight to her perfect C-cup breasts. A soft moan escaped her as I fondled her and took her hardened peaks between my fingers. Moving my hand down and around her waist, I gently lay her on the bed and let my tongue explore her neck. She tasted sweet and I couldn't wait to see what she had to offer down below.

While my lips explored her neck, my hand traveled down her torso and down the front of her panties. She was unbelievably wet already and my cock was throbbing with anticipation. As soon as I dipped a finger inside her, her hands tangled through my hair as she moaned with pleasure. I explored her insides, finding her G-spot, which threw her into a rapid orgasm. I couldn't wait any longer to taste what was waiting for me.

My tongue circled her breasts, paying attention to her hardened nipples as I took each one in my mouth. I took her arms and placed them over her head as I interlaced our fingers tightly together while I made my way down the rest of her body, until I reached her pussy. Letting go of her hands, I placed mine firmly on her hips. With my head between her legs, my mouth explored her. She gasped and moaned while her hands tangled through my hair. I couldn't wait any longer. I needed to bury myself deep inside her. Standing up, I stripped out of my clothes and rolled on a condom. Hovering over her, I slowly placed the head of my cock at her opening, and in one thrust, I was inside. Her pussy greeted me with pleasure and the warmth that enveloped me was incredible. I moved slowly at first with gentle strokes, just to make sure I didn't hurt her. My mouth was clamped around hers and her legs were wrapped tightly around my waist. I picked up the pace and the sensual sounds coming from her heightened. Placing one hand on the headboard and gripping it tight, I thrust in and out of her as the intensity of both our orgasms grew.

"Fuck, you feel so good," I moaned.

Her legs tightened around me as she came and a warmth washed over my cock. One more pump and I halted, straining and moaning as I released every last drop of come I had inside me. I let go of the headboard and collapsed on top of her. Our hearts were rapidly beating as our breath struggled to get back to normal. Her arms tightened around me as I lay there and panic began to set in.

Climbing off her, I went into the bathroom and disposed of the condom. Pulling on my underwear, I went to the living area and sat down on the couch.

"Are you okay?" Zoey asked as she stood in the doorway of the bedroom holding the white sheet up against her.

"I'm fine." I placed my elbows on my knees and rubbed the back of my head. "We better get some sleep. Good night, Zoey," I spoke as I lay down on the couch.

"Sure. Good night, Mr. Grayson."

"Stop with the 'Mr. Grayson.' Just call me Carter."

She gave me a nod, turned around, and climbed into bed.

****

Zoey

I felt it, and so did he. I knew he did. I could sense it while we made love. Our souls connected and I felt as if I'd known him my whole life. My body still trembled and he was by far the best sex I'd ever experienced. This wouldn't change anything and he proved it by going on the couch. I was a fool to think that we'd share the same bed, at least for tonight. He was different when we made love. I felt a tenderness inside him, and the darkness that drowned him was washed away for a short period of time. I needed to get some sleep, because come tomorrow, I would have to deal with the aftermath of what had just happened between us.

I lay in the hospital bed, waiting for Dr. Benson to come back, when I heard a boy crying behind the next curtain.

"His leg is broken in three places. We're going to have to do surgery and put some pins in. Are his parents here yet?"

"They're on their way, doctor."

"Sit tight. We're going to get you prepped for surgery as soon as your parents get here."

"But it hurts!" the boy wailed.

"I know it does. We'll get you something for the pain."

As I lay there, staring at the curtain that separated us, the only thing I could hear were the cries that came from him. Getting up out of bed, I walked over to the curtain and peeked around it before approaching his bedside. He was in so much pain and agony. I felt this overwhelming need to touch him, and when I placed my hand on his, an electrical sensation tore through me.

"You're going to be okay. I promise," I spoke.

His teary eyes stared into mine. "Where did you come from?"

"From the other side of the curtain. I know it hurts, but it won't hurt for much longer," I softly spoke. "What happened to you?"

"I was driving with my best friend Andy and his mom when a truck hit us. Can you try to find my friend Andy?" the boy asked me. "They brought him and his mom in by ambulance."

I looked over and saw a boy standing in the corner staring at us. When the boy saw that I could see him, he spoke to me.

"Tell him to stay cool and not give Miss Harper a hard time anymore." He smiled. *"Tell him that he was the best friend I ever had and he's going to be okay. I have to go now. Please tell him."*

"Oh my god, Carter!" a woman cried as she and a man came running into the room.

I gasped as I jolted up in bed, my heart rapidly beating. It was him. The boy behind the curtain next to me, on that day, was Carter Grayson. I was drenched in sweat as I tried to calm my racing heart.

"Are you okay?" Carter spoke as he turned on the light in the bedroom.

"I'm fine. I'm sorry if I woke you."

"I was just in the bathroom and I heard you. Did you have a nightmare?"

I stared at him as my racing heart began to calm down.

"Something like that. I'm fine. Go back to sleep," I spoke.

He turned and went back on the couch. The feeling that I had when he touched me in his kitchen that one night was the same feeling as when I touched him for the first time in the hospital as a child. The same feeling I had never felt with anyone else before.

I was restless the rest of the night, so I got up at the crack of dawn, quietly got dressed, and walked down to the beach. I stood there as the sun started to rise over the lake and mountains, still thinking about the dream I had last night. Only it wasn't a dream, it was a memory from that day. We met that day when he was in excruciating pain, and then again, all these years later. He was still in pain, but this time, it was a different kind of pain.

Chapter Twenty-Three

Carter

I got up from the couch and noticed the cottage was quiet. Glancing over to the bedroom, I saw that Zoey wasn't there or in the bathroom. Walking over to the window that provided a spectacular view of the lake, I saw her standing by the water with her hands tucked into the pockets of a light jacket she was wearing. She was probably overthinking what happened between us last night, even though I made it very clear that it meant nothing. I put on a sweatshirt, made two cups of coffee, and walked down to where she was standing.

"Morning," I spoke as I handed her a coffee cup.

"Morning. Thank you. You missed the sunrise."

"I bet it was nice," I spoke as I sipped my coffee.

"It was incredible. Look at this view. All this nature and the mountains."

"I will admit it's pretty. Do you want to talk about your nightmare last night?" I asked as I stared out at the lake.

"No. It wasn't even a nightmare. It was more of a memory from my childhood."

"It must have been a bad memory to make you react the way you did."

"It wasn't bad. It was just something I had forgotten about. We need to do that." She pointed out to a couple who was kayaking in the lake.

"Why?" I asked.

"So we can scatter Nora's ashes."

"Why can't we scatter them right here?"

"Really?" She glanced over at me. "Are you just going to stand here and dump them all in one spot and risk them getting blown on shore? If we take a kayak out far enough, we can scatter them where it's nothing but water."

I sighed. "We really need to get on the road to Sedona. Have you forgotten how long of a drive it is?"

"No, I haven't. But do you really want to do this half-assed?" Her brow raised.

"I'll go shower and then we can head to the lobby to find out where we can rent one. But we're going to need to hurry because it's already seven thirty. I want to be on the road by nine."

After I quickly showered and got dressed, Zoey and I took our bags to the lobby and had the desk hold them for us until after our little kayaking adventure. We walked out to the back of the hotel and down the beach, where we found the rental place.

"Do you want our all-day rental?" the guy behind the counter asked.

"No. We'll only be out there about a half hour."

"Oh." He looked at me strangely.

After I paid and signed the paperwork, I asked Zoey, "You do know how to kayak, right?"

"How hard can it be?"

"You've never done this before?" I asked with irritation.

"No."

"For fuck sakes." I shook my head and sighed. "You'll sit in the front and I'll sit in the back. All you have to do is paddle from side to side and we need to do it in unison. Understand?"

"Okay. No problem."

We climbed into the kayak and began paddling out.

"Like this?" Zoey asked from up front.

"Yes. Just like that."

Before long, Zoey was out of unison and our paddles were clashing.

"Zoey!" I shouted.

"Sorry."

A small smile crossed my face as I watched her from behind.

Once we were far enough out, we stopped paddling and I opened the backpack I had stored in the kayak. Taking out urn number one, I held it in my hands, finding it difficult to move.

"It's okay, Carter. This is what she wanted," Zoey spoke.

"I know. Just give me a second."

I took in a deep breath and tipped the urn so it was over the water.

"Paddle, Zoey," I spoke.

She did as I asked, and as the kayak started to slowly move, a light wind swept over not only us, but also Nora's ashes and spread them over parts of the lake.

"Rest in peace, baby sister," I whispered.

****

Zoey

I smiled as I looked a few feet in front of the kayak and saw Nora standing on the water. I turned and glanced at Carter as he sat there and held the urn.

"Do you think she's happy?" he asked.

"Yes. I do," I replied.

He stared at me, and to my surprise, a small smile crossed his lips. It was in that moment that a tiny piece of the darkness that shrouded him began to fade. I turned and looked at Nora, who was still standing there.

"Thank you," she whispered.

I smiled as she faded into the distance.

"I think we should head back and get on the road," Carter spoke.

"Sounds like a plan."

We both picked up our paddles and began paddling back to shore. By time we returned the kayak, grabbed our bags from the hotel, and loaded the SUV, it was nine thirty. As soon as we both climbed in and shut the door, Carter sat there with his hands gripping the steering wheel.

"What's wrong?" I asked.

He slowly turned his head and looked at me.

"I don't know. I just have this weird feeling that maybe we should go back inside the hotel and eat breakfast before we leave."

"We're already a half hour behind," I spoke.

"I'm aware of that, Zoey."

"Then let's go. I'm starving."

We climbed out of the SUV and went inside to the Sierra Café.

"Table for two," Carter spoke to the hostess.

We followed her to our table, took our seats, and looked over the breakfast menu. After placing our order, I wrapped my hands around the white coffee cup and stared at Carter while he made a phone call to his office. He was so handsome and I couldn't stop thinking about what happened last night. No one had ever made me feel the way he did in those moments and it scared me. It scared me because I knew, in some way, we belonged together and that was something he'd never see. Not until he put closure on Angelique and his baby's death.

Chapter Twenty-Four

Carter

Shortly after I hung up with Ross, our food came and I told Zoey we needed to eat quickly so we could get on the road and head to Sedona. I was worried about the time, so I called the Enchantment Resort, explained our situation, and ended up booking another night just in case. Zoey sat across from me and her eyes burned brightly into mine.

"What?" I asked.

"I'm just wondering how you're doing, that's all. I know it's hard to scatter Nora's ashes."

"I'm doing fine. I really have no choice. Do I?"

"If you want to talk about it—"

"Dammit, Zoey. I don't want to talk about it. Why the fuck are you always trying to get me to open up? It's not who I am, so leave it alone," I spoke a little too loud and the two old ladies at the next table looked over at us.

"Okay," she softly spoke and continued to eat her breakfast.

The rest of the time spent at the café was quiet. I had pissed Zoey off. I could tell because she wouldn't look at me. But she needed to understand that I wouldn't or never would talk about anything. As soon as I paid the bill, we climbed into the SUV and headed to Sedona. We were about five miles in when suddenly we hit a traffic jam.

"What the hell is this?" I sighed.

"I see sirens up ahead. It looks like an accident."

"Great." I threw my hands up. "Just fucking great. At this rate, we're never going to get to Sedona."

After a while, traffic started to slowly move, and when we got up to where the accident was, Zoey rolled down the window and asked the police officer when it happened.

"Excuse me. When did this accident happen?"

"About an hour ago," the officer responded.

"Thank you." She rolled her window up.

"Why did you want to know when the accident happened?" I asked her.

"Remember that weird feeling you had, so we ended up going back into the hotel for breakfast?"

"Yeah?"

"Describe it for me, please."

"What?" I frowned at her.

"Describe that feeling you had, because you were so adamant about getting on the road."

"I don't know." I sighed. "I was hungry and I figured you were too. What exactly are you trying to say?"

"Nothing really." She shrugged. "You had a weird feeling so we stayed back, and because we stayed back, we weren't involved in the accident that probably happened at the precise time we were going to be on that road."

"So you're saying if we didn't stay and eat breakfast, we would have been the ones in the accident?"

"Yes. That's exactly what I'm saying. Fate intervened."

I sighed as I tightly gripped the steering wheel.

"There you go again, talking all that nonsense. I don't believe in fate and I don't believe in intuition. I'm going to ask you one last time, Zoey, just stop with all the bullshit because it's really getting on my nerves," I shouted.

I glanced over at her as she stared at me with tears in her eyes. I shook my head and looked straight ahead as I drove on the highway. Damn it.

"Can you pull over, please?" she asked.

"Why?" I glanced over at her.

"Just pull over, Carter," she snapped.

I sighed heavily as I pulled onto the shoulder of the highway. Zoey opened the door and climbed out.

"What the fuck are you doing?" I yelled before she slammed the door shut and began walking along the shoulder.

I waited for a couple cars to pass and then I climbed out and went after her.

"Zoey, stop right now. Turn around and get back in the car!" I shouted.

"Leave me alone, Carter. I just need some space for a few minutes."

"What? We're in the middle of the highway. You can't have space for a few minutes! Get back in the car. You're setting us more behind than we already are!"

She ignored me, and I grew angrier the further she walked away.

"Fine! You want space." I threw my hands up in the air. "You got it, Zoey!"

I walked backed to the SUV and climbed inside. Laying my head back on the headrest, I closed my eyes and took in a deep breath. A few moments later, I heard the door open and Zoey climbed inside.

"Are you finished having your tantrum?" I asked.

She glared at me and pursed her lips.

"I think it's best if neither one of us speaks to each other the rest of the trip," she spoke.

"I agree, but that will be totally impossible."

"Nothing is impossible." She placed her earbuds in her ears.

I drove for the next three hours in silence before Zoey removed her earbuds and spoke, "I have to pee."

"I'll get off at the next exit. Are you hungry?" I asked.

"No," she spoke with a slight attitude in her tone.

We pulled into the first restaurant we saw, got out of the car, and headed inside so we both could use the bathroom.

"Excuse me," an older woman stopped me.

"Yes?"

"Are you a paying customer? Our bathrooms are for paying customers only."

Was this woman serious?

I reached in my pocket and pulled out a hundred-dollar bill.

"Will this do?" I asked.

"That will do just fine." She smiled as she ripped the bill from my hand.

After I was finished using the bathroom, I walked out and didn't see Zoey anywhere.

"Did you see the woman I walked in with come out of the ladies' room?" I asked the older woman.

"She went back outside. She's a sweet girl. I gave her a bag of our homemade chocolate chip cookies."

"Thank you."

I climbed into the SUV and pulled out of the parking lot. Zoey opened the bag of cookies and took one out.

"Those were some really expensive cookies." I smirked.

She glanced over at me and didn't say a word.

"Are they good?" I asked.

"Yep," she replied.

"May I have one?"

Chapter Twenty-Five

Zoey

I tossed the bag onto his lap. He could get his own cookie if he wanted one. He had pushed me to my limits. I was a reasonable and forgiving person, but him—he was an asshole, plain and simple. Just when I thought I poked a tiny hole in the darkness that surrounded him, he found a way to close up that hole. So, I thought it was best that we didn't interact for a while. Everything I said was wrong in his eyes. He was closed off to the point of no return and that was what I needed to accept. It was six p.m. when we arrived in Las Vegas.

"I think we should stop, grab some dinner, and walk around for a bit. My legs are starting to cramp up. It's only a four-and-a-half-hour drive to Sedona from here. Sound good?" He glanced at me.

"Sure," I quietly spoke.

He pulled up to the valet at the Bellagio Hotel.

"There's a restaurant in here called Fix. They have amazing food," he spoke.

We climbed out of the SUV and headed inside. The minute we walked into the lobby of the hotel, I stopped and looked around, taking in the beauty and the excitement that was all around me.

"Have you ever been to Vegas?" Carter asked.

"No. This place is really crowded. Are you sure we'll be able to get a table?"

"We'll get a table." He smirked.

When we reached the restaurant, the hostess with the short black hair, low-cut, cleavage-revealing tight shirt, and short black skirt greeted us with a smile.

"Do you have a reservation?"

"Actually, I don't, but the name is Carter Grayson."

"Oh. Welcome, Mr. Grayson. Is it just the two of you?"

"Yes." He smiled.

"Follow me."

She grabbed two large leather-bound menus and led us to a booth in the corner. He obviously was well known here.

"Good evening, Mr. Grayson." A tall man with salt and pepper hair smiled as he filled our water glasses. "It's good to see you again."

"Good evening, George. Good to see you as well."

"Double scotch on the rocks?" he asked.

"Please."

"And for you, Madame?"

"A glass of Pinot, please."

He gave me a slight nod and walked away. I looked around the restaurant. Dark wood floors and a mixture of tables and booths to match filled the place. The ambience was cozy. A dark setting with subtle lighting and candles that flickered in the center of the tables. George, our waiter, brought our drinks, set them down in front of us, and proceeded to take our order. After Carter handed him our menus, he picked up his glass and kicked back more than half his scotch while he stared at me.

"Listen, Zoey. I'm sorry for what I said earlier. This cold shoulder bullshit needs to stop."

I picked up my glass of wine and sipped it as I glared at him.

"You think I'm crazy and you've made it known several times. So, let me tell you what I think about you and then we can put it behind us and move on."

"Fair enough," he spoke.

"I think you are a mean, arrogant, and miserable man. You're rude, condescending, and just an overall jerk. You're very disrespectful and I don't appreciate it."

I could see the look of anger wash over his face as he held his drink in his hand.

"Okay. I think you're crazy and you think I'm a total disrespectful asshole. Now that we understand each other, we can move forward," he spoke as he finished his drink.

George walked over and placed our plates in front of us.

"Another drink, Mr. Grayson?"

"Yes, please."

I picked up my fork and knife and cut into my filet.

"Are we good now?" Carter asked.

"Sure. We're good," I spoke without looking at him.

"What do you think of the place?" he asked.

"It seems you're well known here."

"I'm in Vegas a lot and this is where I stay. I also own a few properties here. One of which I'm in the process of buying."

"You've really made a success for yourself," I spoke. "I mean, you're young and to have what you do at your age is incredible."

"Thanks. My work is my life. It's all I have and it's all I ever will have."

"There's more to life than work, Carter," I spoke without hesitation, even though I knew it would set him off.

"I actually believed that at one time, but not anymore." He picked up his drink and threw it back down his throat.

We finished our dinner without saying too much to each other. After Carter paid the bill, we left the restaurant and headed to the lobby of the hotel to leave, when noticed a large group of people standing around a man who was lying on the floor. One person was screaming to call 911. I made my way through the crowd and knelt down beside him.

"I'm a nurse. Everyone needs to stand back," I shouted.

He wasn't breathing, so I started CPR.

"Does anyone know what happened?" I asked.

"He was just standing there, grabbed his chest, and went down," a man spoke.

"Come on. Come back to us," I spoke as I continued the chest compressions.

"Oh my God, Henry!" A hysterical woman came running and grabbed his hand.

I continued the chest compressions and breathing into his mouth. Suddenly, I felt a hand on my shoulder behind me. When I turned around, it was him.

"Thank you for trying to save me, sweetheart, but it's my time to go. Tell my beautiful wife, Angie, that I love her with all my heart and that I'll be watching over her. Also tell her that everything she's going to need is locked in the wall safe in our bedroom and the combination is taped under the drawer of my nightstand."

A sadness settled inside me as I stopped the compressions and looked at his wife. Suddenly, the paramedics came through with the stretcher and knelt down beside his body.

"He's gone," I spoke to them. "I did everything I could."

"No!" Angie screamed.

I stood, walked over to her, placed my arm around her shoulder, and helped her up.

"He told me to tell you that he loves you with all his heart and that he'll be watching over you."

She looked at me with her tear-filled eyes. "What?"

"He thanked me for trying to save him, but he said it was his time. I'm so sorry. He also wanted you to know that everything you're going to need is locked in the wall safe in your bedroom and the combination is taped under the drawer of his nightstand."

She placed her hand on my cheek as the tears steadily flowed from her eyes.

"Thank you," she whispered.

"You're welcome." I gave her a tender small smile.

I looked across the crowd and saw Carter walking my way. I wiped my brow as he approached me.

"Are you okay?" He lightly touched my arm.

"Can we just go, please?"

"Sure."

I turned around and walked out the door. Carter handed the valet his ticket and we stood there waiting for them to bring the car around.

"I'm sorry you couldn't save him, Zoey," he spoke in a low voice.

"Me too."

The car pulled up to the curb and Carter opened the door for me.

"Thanks." I gave him a small smile as I climbed inside.

Chapter Twenty-Six

Carter

Zoey was visibly upset and I really didn't know what to say to her. I pulled out of the hotel parking lot and headed towards the highway.

"As long as this drive goes smooth and we don't run into any problems, we should be in Sedona around twelve thirty a.m."

She sat there, looking straight ahead, and didn't say a word.

"You did everything you could for that man," I spoke.

"I know." She looked out the passenger window. "It was his time, and when it's your time, there's nothing anyone can do."

"And you know that for a fact?" I cautiously asked, knowing she was going to spew out some type of bullshit.

"Yes. He told me."

"What do you mean 'he told' you?" I glanced over at her.

"I'm not going to explain it, Carter, and you won't understand. All you'll do is call me crazy and start yelling and I'm in no mood for it. I'll drive the rest of the way in a couple of hours."

This feeling inside me emerged. There was a sadness in her voice when she said I'd called her crazy and it made me feel—

"I'm sorry for calling you crazy, Zoey. It's just—"

"It's just you, Carter, feeling sorry for yourself because of the tragedies you experienced. You became a victim of circumstance and you locked yourself up in your own little world that consists of nothing but pain and anger. You refuse to see any type of good in anyone or anything. So, if you don't mind, I don't want to talk about what I see all the time, every day, and every minute of my life," she spoke in anger. "You aren't the only person in the world who has lost the people you love. You aren't the only one whose life was affected by tragedy. You just chose to deal with it in a really shitty way."

I immediately swerved and pulled over on the side of the highway, clenching the steering wheel so tight that my knuckles were turning white.

"And who the fuck have you lost?" I screamed at her. "Because from what I can see, you have a perfect little life. You seem content being surrounded by death and sadness all the time. So yeah, you're fucking crazy!"

By the light of the moon that framed her face in the passenger seat, I could see a stream of tears falling from her eyes. She didn't speak a word, but only sat there, staring straight ahead at the darkness. Fuck. I reached over and wiped away the tears that fell down her cheek.

"Don't," she whispered. "Just don't."

"I'm sorry. I know you don't believe me, but I am."

I put the SUV in drive and pulled back onto the highway. The next three hours were nothing but silence. We were getting really good at that.

****

I pulled into the Enchantment Resort at approximately twelve forty-five a.m. Zoey had been asleep for about a half hour and I hated waking her.

"Zoey, we're here," I quietly spoke.

She opened her eyes, sat up straight, and looked around. I dropped her and our bags off at the front door while I parked the SUV since the valet was closed.

"Can I help you?" the older gentleman behind the desk asked.

"Reservation for Carter Grayson."

"Ah yes, Mr. Grayson. We're happy you've arrived."

"Thank you. It's been a long drive." I spoke.

"Your two-bedroom suite is ready and I can call someone to help you with your bags."

"No need. We can take them up ourselves."

"Very well. You will be in suite 325." He politely smiled.

Zoey and I stepped into the elevator, and as soon the doors closed, I looked over at her.

"I'm exhausted. You must be too," I spoke to try and lighten the tension between us.

But she wasn't having any type of conversation with me. She stared straight at the closed doors, gripping the handle of her suitcase tight. I sighed as the doors opened.

"I believe we're this way." I pointed to the left.

We approached room 325 and as soon as I slid the keycard into the lock, I held open the door and motioned for her to step in first.

Chapter Twenty-Seven

Zoey

The moment I stepped into the large suite, the lights automatically turned on. I wheeled my suitcase behind me as I looked around. It was beautiful with beige painted walls, wood beam ceilings, and décor that was casual but sophisticated at the same time. The living area had a beehive fireplace that sat quaintly in the corner, a wall-mounted TV, an oversized couch and chair that were in a deep brown rich leather, and a beautiful wood coffee table to match. There was a kitchen area with a large oak table, oak cabinets, and black speckled granite counter tops. The best part of the room was the sliding glass door that led out to a large wooden deck, which housed a gas grill, a small round wood table, and matching chairs. The view that sat in front of me was breathtaking. Even though it was dark outside, the lights from all over the resort lit up the beautiful scenic box canyon.

"Wow, this is beautiful," Carter spoke as he stood beside me.

I hadn't forgotten what he said and I hadn't forgiven him either. I was tired and speaking to him was the last thing I wanted to do. I walked away, grabbed my suitcase, and wheeled it into the bedroom that had two double beds.

"You can have the room with the king-size bed," Carter spoke from the doorway.

"No. This is fine. Now if you'll excuse me, I'm going to bed." I walked over and shut the door in his face.

After changing into my nightshirt and washing my face, I turned off the light in the bathroom. As I stepped into the bedroom, a cold sensation tore through me. I looked around but didn't see anyone, which was strange.

"I don't know what else to do," I quietly spoke as I climbed into bed.

The moment my head hit the pillow, I was out.

****

I opened my eyes as the sun poured through the large window. Looking around the room, I had forgotten for a moment where I was. Letting out a long yawn, I picked up my phone from the nightstand and saw that it was nine a.m. I hadn't a clue what time Carter planned on leaving for the Grand Canyon, so I took a shower, got dressed, and ventured into the kitchen area for some coffee. I wasn't sure if he was up yet, and to be honest, I really wasn't ready to see him after last night.

I popped a k-cup into the Keurig machine that was sitting in the corner on the granite countertop. Looking around the suite, I didn't see or hear any sign of him. I was sure he was still asleep. I took my coffee out to the wooden deck and sat down in one of the chairs that faced the canyon. There was something about this place that filled me with peace.

I had just finished my coffee when I heard the sliding door open. I turned around and saw a very sweaty Carter Grayson standing on the deck.

"Morning," he spoke as he wiped his face with a small white towel.

"I thought you were still asleep."

"Nah. I was up at the crack of dawn, so I decided to go for a run."

"How was it?" I asked as my eyes stared straight ahead.

He took the seat beside me and chugged a bottle of water he was holding.

"Good. It's beautiful here. I would have asked you to come, but—"

"I wouldn't have gone anyway," I interrupted him. "You couldn't have gotten much sleep."

"I didn't. The bed was a little too comfortable." He smirked. "Go figure. Anyway, I brought you something back. It's inside on the counter. Maybe you should go take a look."

I narrowed my eye at him for a moment before getting up from my seat and stepping back inside. Over on the counter sat a white square medium-sized box.

"What's in here?" I asked him.

"Open the lid and find out."

I slowly lifted the cardboard lid with my fingers and inside the box sat a huge, probably the biggest I'd ever seen, round donut with white icing and the words "I'm sorry" written in pink on it.

"I don't think I'd ever seen a donut this big before. Where did you get this?" I looked at him with a smile on my lips.

"The bakery in the hotel had them. I remember you telling Nora that your favorite donuts were the ones with the white frosting."

"And you had them put this writing on it?" I asked.

"Yeah. I'm sorry for what I said to you yesterday, Zoey. I was out of line. There are just some things you don't understand."

"I know you don't believe me, Carter, but I do understand. In fact, I'm probably the only person in the world who does."

"There's no way you could," he spoke. "We have a long trip ahead of us still and I don't want there to be any tension. So, I'm extending an olive branch, or donut." He smiled.

I couldn't help but smile back.

"Okay. I accept your apology. How about we cut this donut in half and eat it?"

"Sounds good to me."

He walked over to the drawer, opened it and pulled out a knife.

"Shall I do the honor?" He held the knife up.

"Be my guest." I nodded with a smile.

He cut the donut in half and it was still too big, so he cut it into fours.

Chapter Twenty-Eight

Carter

Even though I was dead tired, I was up all night replaying the shouting match Zoey and I had in the car. She was right about me living in my own world of pain and anger and how I refused to see any type of good in anyone or anything. Most of that was true, but I did see good in her, too much good and that was what frightened me so much. She told me that I wasn't the only one whose life was affected by tragedy, insinuating that she too had suffered some in her life. I kept going back to when we were at the gas station and she let it slip about her mother. But why the hell would she keep that from me? After tossing and turning, I decided to go for a run because it always helped clear my head. But this time, it didn't. It only made me have more questions about her. There was a mystery surrounding Zoey Benson and there was something she didn't want me to know. The words "I don't want to talk about what I see all the time, every day, and every minute of my life" circled around in my head. I had a feeling she wasn't talking about her terminally ill patients, and I was going to find out exactly what she meant, whether I wanted to know the truth or not. I needed to find out what kind of person I was dealing with.

I took our large pieces of donuts and sat down at the table while Zoey made us each a coffee.

"What time do you want to head out for the Grand Canyon?" she asked as she set our coffee cups down on the table.

"After I shower," I spoke as I picked up my coffee and took a sip. "I have a question for you, Zoey."

"Sure. What is it?" she asked as she took a bite of her donut.

"Right before Nora passed away, you told her you could see my parents like she said she did. Was that really true or were you just saying that for her sake?"

I could see the hesitation on her face and silence crossed her lips. I reached over and lightly placed my hand on hers.

"It's okay. You can tell me the truth and I promise not to judge you or say anything out of line."

"As much as I want to believe you, Carter, I'm not going to answer your question."

She pulled her hand out from under mine and picked up her coffee cup.

"And why not?" I narrowed my eye at her.

"Because you aren't ready to hear the truth."

"Who are you to decide if I'm ready or not?" I spoke with irritation.

"You already think I'm crazy as it is. I'm not about to add anything else to that."

I sat there, eating my donut and sipping my coffee while staring at her. If she was mentally ill by some means, then I wouldn't have to worry about wanting to be with her. She was complicated and that was something I didn't need in my life.

"Are you on any kind of medication?" I asked her.

Her brow arched as her eyes stared into mine.

"Have you ever seen me take any medication?"

"No, but I don't know if you take something right before you go to bed or not."

"Mr. Grayson, what exactly are you insinuating?"

"I know you're adopted, so maybe mental illness runs in your family."

She threw her head back and a roar of laughter escaped her.

"You think I have a mental illness? Wow. Okay, we're going to settle this once and for all because, honestly, I'm tired of you and your accusations." She got up from her seat and took her plate and coffee cup over to the sink. "I can see dead people, aka, ghosts, spirits, or whatever you want to call them. Plain and simple. I'm not crazy. They're real and I can't help it. So, to answer your question from earlier, yes, I did see your parents standing by Nora's bed and she saw them too. And by the way, I see Nora every now and again. She was with us while we were scattering her ashes in Lake Tahoe. And the man at the hotel, yes, he was standing behind me because he needed me to give a message to his wife. Now, if you'll excuse me, I'm going to take my crazy ass to the bedroom. Just let me know when you're ready to leave. Or, if you'd prefer, I can catch a plane home and you can handle the rest of this by yourself. I wouldn't want you to be freaked out or have to deal with my craziness any more. I know Nora wanted me to help you, but frankly, it's not worth it anymore. You're beyond help, Mr. Grayson." She began to walk away and then stopped and turned around. "My parents were killed in a plane crash when I was five years old. So yeah, my life has been affected by tragedies as well." She stormed off and into the bedroom where she slammed the door shut.

I sat there, slowly closed my eyes for a moment, and tried to process everything she just told me. I didn't want to believe her. She had lied to me about her parents from the beginning and she was lying about everything else. I'd had enough, so I got up from the table, went to her room, and opened the door in a fit of rage.

"You are a liar!" I pointed at her. "You lied about your parents and you're lying about everything else. Did you just make up that bullshit about them being killed in a plane crash to make yourself feel better from being abandoned?" I shouted. "I'm calling the airlines and sending you home. I can't deal with you anymore."

She sat on the edge of the bed and stared at me while I yelled. She didn't move and she didn't speak a word. In fact, she didn't do a goddamn thing. She didn't even flinch. Just as I was about to shut the door, she spoke.

"Year 1997. New York. Flight 4211. Kenneth and Margo Anderson."

I slowly shook my head at her, shut the door, and went to my room. Pulling my phone from my pocket, I called the airlines to book her a flight back to New York.

"What the hell do you mean no flights are going into New York?"

"I'm sorry, sir, but both LaGuardia and JFK have experienced severe power outages and we aren't sure when it will be restored. Electric crews are telling us maybe sometime tomorrow."

"You have got to be fucking kidding me."

"I wish I was, sir. Thousands of passengers are stranded at the moment and a ton of flights have been canceled. My advice would be to check back tomorrow."

"Thank you."

In a fit of anger, I threw my phone on the bed and climbed into the shower. When I was finished and got dressed, I picked up my phone and called my private investigator.

"Carter, how are you, my friend?"

"Hey, Charlie. I need a favor."

"Sure, man, what's up?"

"Can you see what you can dig up on a plane crash back in 1997? Apparently, there was one in New York, Flight 4211."

"I think I remember that. Give me a few hours and I'll call you back."

"Thanks, Charlie."

After ending the call, I went back to Zoey's room and opened the door.

"Don't you know it's rude to enter someone's room without knocking?" she spoke.

"I paid for the room, so technically, I can do whatever the fuck I want. I called the airlines and apparently there are no flights going in or out of New York right now due to some major power outage at both airports. So we better get on the road to the Grand Canyon and I'll call again in the morning."

"I don't want to go with you." She folded her arms.

"I don't care. You're not staying here by yourself. Nora wanted you to come on the trip and since you're here and can't go anywhere else, you're going to help me scatter her ashes over the fucking Grand Canyon!" I sternly spoke. "So let's go!"

Chapter Twenty-Nine

Zoey

He walked away and I looked around the room.

"Really? Power outages in both airports? Come on. Why the hell are you doing this to me?"

I took in a deep breath, grabbed my purse, and followed him outside to the SUV. The drive to the Grand Canyon was probably the longest drive of my life. Even though it was only supposed to be an hour and a half drive, the GPS took us a different way, which extended our time by forty-five minutes. Needless to say, Carter was not happy.

We drove along Desert View Drive and stopped at Grandview Point. It was terribly crowded.

"What the hell," Carter spoke.

"Keep driving to Moran Point. It's a few miles down the road."

"And you think there will be any less people there?" he spoke with an irritated tone.

"It doesn't matter about the people. It's where we have to go."

"Let me guess, Nora told you to go there?" he spoke with sarcasm.

I didn't reply. I just rolled my eyes and stared out the window. When we reached Moran Point, Carter immediately found a spot to park the SUV. We both climbed out, grabbed one of the urns, and walked the trail up to the point where we were lucky enough to find a spot where nobody was. Once we reached the top, I stood there and looked out into the picturesque wonder that sat before me.

"Wow. This is like something out of a painting," Carter spoke as he held the urn against his chest.

"It's beautiful. No wonder Nora wanted this to be one of her resting places," I said.

Carter removed the lid from the urn and held it over the edge for a moment before slowly tipping it forward and letting the ashes fall over the depth of the canyon.

"Rest in peace, Nora," he spoke.

I looked over at Carter, and standing next to him was his sister, smiling as she watched her ashes scatter. She lightly placed her hand on his shoulder. He looked over and then at me.

"What?" I asked.

"Nothing," he spoke with a bit of panic.

He placed the lid back on the urn and took a seat on the ground. We both sat there in silence for about thirty minutes, taking in the beauty that nature had formed.

"I think we should grab something to eat and head back to Sedona," Carter spoke.

We drove for about an hour and pulled into a restaurant called The Steak House. After we were seated, Carter's phone rang.

"Excuse me, I need to take this," he spoke as he got up from his seat and walked away. A few moments later, he returned, sat down in his chair, and stared at me with a weird look on his face.

"Is everything okay?" I asked.

"Yeah. It was just business," he spoke as he placed his napkin on his lap.

I could tell something was wrong by his tone of voice.

"Was Nora there with us at the Grand Canyon?" he asked.

"I don't know," I lied.

"I swear I felt a hand on my shoulder while we were standing there. You said she was with us in Lake Tahoe. So, if you were telling the truth, then you would have seen her at the Grand Canyon. So, please, Zoey, tell me the truth."

"I don't know, Carter. I didn't see anyone."

There was no way I was going to tell him in the middle of the restaurant. This man was a ticking time bomb and I wasn't about to set him off.

"Okay." He took a sip of his water. "Is there anything you want to talk about?" he asked.

"No."

"Why not?"

I looked at him in disbelief. Just a few hours ago, he was believing I had a mental illness, called me a liar, and tried to send me home. So why the hell would I want to talk to him about anything? He had some nerve asking me that and going about as if he did nothing wrong. He'd said a lot of things to me since the first day we'd met and I had chosen to overlook ninety-nine percent of them, but what he said about me lying about my parents to make myself feel better for being abandoned crossed the line and that was something I couldn't overlook or forgive him for.

"I have nothing to say to you, Mr. Grayson."

He took in a sharp breath and sat back in his chair.

"This is because of earlier, isn't it? I'm sorry."

"You're always sorry, but it doesn't change things. You can say you're sorry a million times over, yet you continue to say things that hurt me over and over again. You don't want me on this trip and I don't want to be here. So, tomorrow morning, I'm calling the airlines and getting a flight back home to Connecticut. I'll pick up the rest of my things in a couple of days."

"Fine." He nodded. "If that's what you want."

"It is."

"Fine," he spoke with an attitude.

We finished our dinner in silence and then climbed into the SUV and headed back to the Enchantment Resort.

"That call I took earlier at dinner. It was my private investigator, Charlie. I had him do some digging on that plane crash you told me about," he spoke.

"Good for you." I sighed.

"Everyone on that flight was killed, except for one survivor. A child. A five-year-old girl. But her name was kept out of the papers to protect her identity, and then shortly after the crash, she disappeared. That little girl was you, wasn't it?"

I looked at him as tears filled my eyes, but I couldn't speak. I turned away and looked out the passenger window.

"Zoey, I'm so sorry. I can't even imagine."

He reached his hand over and softly placed it on mine, which was resting on my lap. I pulled away.

"Please talk to me," he spoke in a tender voice.

"Yes. I was the little girl who survived the crash of Flight 4211. The only survivor out of 525 passengers, including my parents." A single tear fell from my eye.

"I don't know what to say to you except how sorry I am."

"Don't be. That was twenty years ago."

He pulled up to the valet at the Enchantment Resort and we climbed out and went to our suite. The moment he opened the door and I stepped inside, I started to go straight to my room, but felt his hand grab my arm and stop me. I looked at his hand and then at him. He pulled me into a tight embrace and I didn't know what to do. He didn't speak a word. He only held me in the middle of the living area.

After a few moments, he broke our embrace and our eyes locked on each other's. He brought his hand up and lightly cupped my chin.

"I don't want you to go home tomorrow. I want you to stay and finish this trip with me. To be honest, I don't think I can do it alone. Please," he spoke in a begging voice.

"You can do this alone, Carter. In fact, I think you need to."

"That's your decision, then?" he asked.

"Yes. I'm sorry." I looked away.

He swallowed hard and walked over to the sliding glass door. Placing his hands in his pockets as he stared out at the beautiful view of the canyon, he spoke, "I understand and there's no need for you to be sorry."

"Thank you," I quietly spoke and went to my room.

Taking my phone from my purse, I called the airport and was able to get on a flight back to Connecticut at eight a.m., which meant I would have to leave the hotel around four thirty, since it was a two-hour drive to the airport.

Chapter Thirty

Carter

She was leaving in the morning and I wasn't happy about it. Knowing what I knew about a piece of her past made me feel an overwhelming sadness for her. There was nothing I could do about it now. I had pushed her away and to the point where she couldn't even finish the trip with me. I didn't blame her one bit, though. I wouldn't want to be around someone like me either. I intentionally did everything I could to make her see that I wasn't who she thought I was. That the man I once was, was gone. I'd let her sleep for tonight, but come morning, I'd ask her one more time to stay and come with me to Seattle. I wasn't looking forward to that drive at all, especially alone.

The next morning, I awoke around seven a.m., quickly took a shower, and went to see if she was up. When I walked into the kitchen area, I saw a white piece of paper sitting on the counter. Picking it up, I held it in my hand and read it.

Carter,

I managed to get on a flight that leaves at eight a.m., so when you read this, I'll already be gone. Please drive safe to Seattle and have a safe flight to Hawaii. You can do this alone. Just remember that this is what Nora wanted and you're doing it for her. Take the time alone and reflect on all the memories that you and Nora made. Remember, memories are a treasure and they were made with love. Embrace them.

Zoey

I took in a deep breath and set the letter down. She was gone already and there wasn't a goddamn thing I could do about it. Anger rose inside me and I needed to get out of here. Grabbing my bags, I checked out of the hotel and told the valet to bring my car around.

"Excuse me, Mr. Grayson," the valet gentleman spoke. "There seems to be a problem with your vehicle."

"What kind of problem?"

"It won't start."

"You're kidding me." I sighed.

"I wish I was. We're going to try to jumpstart it."

"Fine. Can you please hurry? I have to get on the road."

While I stood there waiting, I pulled my phone from my pocket and debated whether or not to text Zoey. What would I say to her? I'm sorry? She didn't believe that anymore.

"Excuse me, Mr. Grayson?"

"Did you get it started?" I asked as I put my phone back in my pocket.

"Unfortunately, we didn't. It won't start. You're going to need to call a tow truck."

"Listen, I need to start heading to Seattle. I don't have time for this shit."

"Is there anything we can do for you?"

"Get me another car!"

"The nearest rental car place is about an hour from here. I can have someone drive you there, but I would call first to make sure they have a vehicle to rent."

"I'll do that, thank you."

I huffed and pulled my phone from my pocket. Looking up the nearest rental car place, I dialed their number only to find out they didn't have one car available for rent.

"How the hell can a rental car company not have a rental car?" I asked in irritation.

"I'm sorry, sir, but this is one of our busiest times of the year. We will have one available in a couple of days if you would like to be put on our list."

"I don't have a couple of days!" I shouted. "Just forget it."

I placed my hand on my head and paced around the lobby of the hotel. Now what the fuck was I going to do? I looked up at the ceiling and spoke, "Sorry, Nora. I have no choice."

I called the airport and was able to get on a flight to Seattle that departed at four forty-five p.m. I did check with the airline I was flying with to make sure there wouldn't be a problem traveling with Nora's ashes. The only requirement they had was that the ashes had to be checked in a luggage bag. So, I headed to the hotel gift shop to see if I could find a box that would fit the ashes and my suitcase since the urn was way too big. After finding the perfect box that had little pink-colored roses on it, I transferred her ashes from the urn and tucked it safely into my suitcase. While I waited for the car service to pick me up, I placed a call to the rental car company and had them send a tow truck to the hotel for the SUV.

After I arrived at the airport and checked in, I decided to grab something to eat since I was going to be stuck here for another four hours, and I was starving. The only thing that sounded good was Panera, since it was only one of three food places in the area that seemed normal. When I walked inside, I scanned the small space to see if there were any tables available. "What the hell?" I spoke to myself.

"Zoey?" I walked over to where she sat.

"Carter! What are you doing here? You're supposed to be on the road to Seattle," she spoke in shock.

"And you are supposed to be back in Connecticut already."

"My flight keeps getting pushed back because of mechanical issues with the plane."

"Well, the SUV wouldn't start, and when I called the rental car company to rent another vehicle, they didn't have any."

"What?" She laughed. "How is that possible?"

"Apparently, it's their busiest time of the year. So I had no choice but to catch a flight to Seattle. It doesn't leave until four forty-five."

"You're stuck here for another four hours?"

"Apparently, I am. How long are you going to be here?"

"I have no clue. Last time I checked, the lady was rude and told me that they'll keep the passengers updated as they get information."

"Would you mind if I sat with you? There doesn't appear to be any open tables."

"Not at all. Did you order your food yet?" she asked.

"No. I'm going to do that now. Can I get you anything?"

"Thanks, but I'm good." She smiled.

I gave her a smile back and went up to the counter to order some food. I couldn't believe she was still here, but I was happy to see her.

Chapter Thirty-One

Zoey

I looked around the area I was sitting in for a sign. Any sign that someone was here watching us. My plane with the mechanical problems and delayed flight status, and Carter's SUV not starting and no rental cars available were more than a coincidence. It was nice to see a familiar face here, even if it was his. He seemed a little bit different today and I couldn't put my finger on why.

"I still can't believe I ran into you here," he spoke as he took the seat across from me.

"I believe it." I smiled.

He gave me an odd look, smiled back, and began eating his sandwich.

"I apologized to Nora in case you're wondering. I told her I didn't have a choice but to fly to Seattle," he spoke.

"Oh, I'm sure she doesn't mind."

"I was a little shocked when I got your letter this morning. I didn't think you'd get such an early flight."

"It was the only one available. I was lucky because there were only two seats left."

"Maybe not so lucky since you're still here." He smirked.

"It's been quite a day so far."

Suddenly, a woman's voice came on the overhead speaker.

"Attention, passengers. Flight 445 to Connecticut has been cancelled. We will have a flight going out tomorrow morning at seven a.m. Please see the attendant at the desk for further instructions and hotel accommodations."

I sat there as I pursed my lips and slowly nodded my head. Was I surprised? Absolutely not.

"Was that your flight they just cancelled?" Carter asked.

"Yep. It sure was."

"Well, I guess you'll just have to fly to Seattle with me." He smirked.

"I don't know, Carter. We just can't seem—"

"It'll be different this time, Zoey. I promise. I really do need you with me for this and I'm really sorry for everything. When you're ready to talk about it, I'd like to get to know you better, and whatever it is you tell me, I'm ready to hear it."

I sat across from him and stared into his eyes, which were a little brighter, and the sincerity in his voice led me to believe he was telling the truth.

"Okay. I'll fly to Seattle with you." I smiled.

"Really? Then we better go get you a ticket. If there aren't any seats available, then we'll find another flight for us."

"Trust me, Carter. There will be a seat available."

He cocked his head and he pursed his lips.

"You seem confident about that."

"I am."

He finished eating his sandwich and we both headed to the ticket counter.

"How may I help you?" The young blonde asked.

"I was supposed to be on the flight to Connecticut that was cancelled. Could you tell me if there are any seats available for the four forty-five flight to Seattle?"

"Let me check for you." She began typing away at her keyboard. "We have one seat available and it's in first class." She smiled.

"She'll take it," Carter spoke. "And I'll pay the difference."

"You're all set. Have a safe trip."

She handed me my ticket and I looked at it.

"What seat are you in?" Carter asked.

"3C"

"I'm in 3A, so we'll be across from each other." He smiled.

"Of course we will be." I grinned. "What did you do about Nora's ashes?"

"I had to buy a box at the gift shop in the hotel and transfer the ashes. The airline said it would be fine as long as I kept them in my checked luggage."

"Good. I'm glad they didn't give you any trouble."

"Would you like to go grab a coffee and sit somewhere until we have to be at our gate?" he asked.

"Sure. Coffee sounds really good right now."

We walked around until we found a Starbucks, ordered our coffees, and then took a seat at a small round table for two right outside the café.

"If you don't mind me asking, how did you end up with John and Scott?"

"Scott was the fireman who found me in the plane and he rode with me in the ambulance to the hospital. John was the attending ER doctor who treated me when I was brought in. The press surrounded the hospital for days. John had a good friend who was pretty high up at Child Protective Services and he let him and Scott take me home with them to hide me until it blew over."

"Didn't you have any other family that could care for you?"

"My mom's parents died about a year before I was born and the only living relative my dad had was his father, who was a major alcoholic."

"You were only five. How did you know all that?"

"My mom told me about her parents and John and Scott told me about my grandfather. They had hired a private investigator because they wanted to adopt me. Because of John's friend and the pull he had, I officially became Zoey Benson two months after the crash."

"What I don't understand, Zoey, is why the story about being left on the church steps?"

I sipped my coffee before answering his question.

"Do you realize what would happen if anyone found out that I was the child who survived that plane crash? About a month after it happened and things were starting to calm down with the press, John and Scott bought a house in Connecticut and we moved there. Even though it wasn't official yet, they introduced me to everyone as their daughter. It was there that we started a new life as a family."

"I suppose you're right. If anyone had caught wind that you were the child who survived, they would have called the press and they would have been all over you. You would never have been able to live a normal life."

I laughed. "My life is far from normal."

"I kind of get that impression. Like I said earlier, when you're ready to talk about it, I'm ready to listen."

I smiled as Carter looked at his watch.

"We need to get to our gate."

As soon as they called first class to start boarding, Carter handed his ticket to the attendant and I followed behind. Just before we boarded, I looked over to the right and saw Nora and Angelique standing there watching as we boarded the plane together. I gave them a small smile.

"Who are you smiling at?" Carter asked as he looked over at me.

"No one. I'm just happy to finally get out of this damn airport."

"You and me both."

Carter took my carry-on and put it in the overhead compartment for me before sitting in his seat.

"Are the two of you together?" the older woman next to him asked.

"Umm. Yes. We are," Carter replied.

"Well, then, she can have my seat." She smiled as she got up.

"Thank you. But this seat is fine," I spoke.

"No. No. I don't mind at all."

"Are you sure?"

"Positive, honey. A window seat is a window seat, right?"

"Right. Thank you."

"You're welcome. A lovely couple as yourselves should be sitting next to one another."

I took the seat next to Carter and buckled my seat belt.

"That was very nice of her to switch seats with you," he spoke. "Our bad day is looking brighter."

"It is. Isn't it?" I yawned.

"Why don't you take a little nap? Feel free to lay your head on my shoulder," he spoke as he grabbed the small red pillow and rested it on his shoulder.

"Thanks." I smiled. "Maybe I will."

I laid my head down on the pillow that rested on his shoulder. He was starting to change, and so far, I was liking what I saw.

Chapter Thirty-Two

Carter

I glanced over at her as she slept on my shoulder. I was growing attached to her and I didn't even fully realize it until I woke up this morning and she was gone. I felt alone, more alone than I already was. I hadn't had feelings like this since Angelique and it scared the hell out of me. I wanted to keep everything buried down in the depths of my soul, but Zoey wouldn't let me and maybe it was time I started to let her inside my world.

We landed in Seattle and we took a cab to the Four Seasons Hotel, where I already had booked us two bay suites with an adjoining door.

"I'm starving. How about dinner and a little exploring of Seattle?" I asked.

"I like that idea. Just give me a second to change."

We headed down to the Goldfinch Tavern, where there was about an hour wait.

"Are you sure about the wait?" I asked the hostess as I slipped her a fifty-dollar bill.

"Umm. Let me double check for you, sir."

A moment later she returned, grabbed two menus, and asked us to follow her.

"Really, Carter?"

"What? I'm starving and I wasn't about to wait another hour."

"We could have gone somewhere else."

"Have you ever been to Seattle?" I asked.

"No."

"Well, let's just say there's long waits all over the city. I'm sure that girl could use fifty bucks." I smirked.

We finished dinner and headed out into the busy and crowded streets of Seattle.

"Take my hand," I spoke as I held it out to her. "As you can see, it's crowded and we're going to have to weave our way through the crowds of people."

She placed her hand in mine and our fingers interlaced. A feeling triggered through my body and the softness of her hand felt good. I took her to Pike Place Market first. She loved it just like I knew she would.

"Oh my gosh, look at these beautiful flowers!" she exclaimed.

"You like flowers?" I asked.

"Of course. Who doesn't? And I just don't like them, I love them. Don't you?" She cocked her head.

"Yeah. Flowers are nice, I guess."

She traced her finger along the delicate petals of a bunch of pink roses that were sitting in a large bucket.

"You guess?" She laughed. "Flowers are a symbol of many things. Because of their beauty and delicate nature, they instantly make people happy. They are treasures and symbols of the memories they represent. Each flower has its own meaning, and what most people don't understand is when they're giving flowers to someone, it's important to know the meaning and symbolism behind each flower. For example, red roses mean love, but this purple rose over here," she pointed, "symbolizes a highly spiritual love such as soul mates. So the purple overrules the red in love."

"I didn't know that," I spoke.

"Most people don't. It's like when people leave the favorite flowers of their loved ones on their graves. It's done as an expression. A way of saying 'I know you're not here anymore, but I still love you.' Make sense?"

"I guess. Can we talk about something else?"

"Yeah. Of course."

We walked around, did some window shopping, and headed back to the hotel. It was already ten thirty and we were both exhausted. When we got back to our rooms, Zoey went in hers and I went in mine. I changed into a pair of sweatpants, took a seat on the edge of the bed, and cupped my face in my hands, thinking about how I wanted her to stay in my bed tonight. Suddenly, there was a knock on the adjoining door. Getting up, I opened it.

"Hey," I spoke.

"Do you by any chance have any bottled water in your mini fridge? Mine is only stocked with alcohol."

"Let's go take a look."

Walking over to the mini fridge, I opened it and took out a bottle of water.

"Thank you," she softly spoke.

"You're welcome."

I stared into her beautiful eyes and brought my hand up to her cheek.

"Thank you for agreeing to come with me. I know things between us haven't been good."

"I really didn't have a choice." She smiled.

I didn't know what she meant by that and I didn't want to because all I wanted to do was kiss her sweet lips. I leaned forward and softly brushed my mouth against hers. She reciprocated, and it was then I knew she didn't want me to stop. I deepened our kiss as her lips parted and my tongue met hers. My hands roamed up and down her beautiful body as my cock became rock hard. I grasped the bottom of her shirt, broke our kiss, and lifted it over her head while our eyes locked on each other's. Reaching behind her, I unclasped her bra with ease and tossed it on the floor. My hands instantly gravitated to her perfect breasts, cupping them and taking her hardened nipples between my fingers. My tongue caressed her collarbone, over each breast and across her torso as I got down on my knees. Unbuttoning her jeans, I slid them and her panties off her hips and down to her ankles where she stepped out of them. My mouth lightly pressed against her lips and my tongue circled her clit. Her fingers tangled through my hair while she let out satisfying groans. I brought my hand up to her opening and slid my finger inside her, feeling the wetness that emerged. She gasped and her legs tightened as she came.

Standing, I picked her up and carried her to my bed, gently laid her down on her back, and took my sweatpants down, kicking them to the side. To my surprise, she sat up on the edge of the bed and wrapped her soft warm hand around my cock, moving it up and down slowly before covering the tip with her lips. I threw my head back and moaned at the sensation that flowed through my body. I didn't want her to stop, but I didn't want to come that way and I was already on the verge. Lightly pushing her back, I hovered over her and kissed her lips while my cock sat in between her legs. One thrust, I was inside and was greeted with a warmth that made my cock tingle with pleasure. Slowly deepening myself inside her, I moaned, as did she. Our lips tangled as I continued to thrust in and out of her at a steady pace. Wrapping my hands around her back, I pulled her up into a sitting position and she moved in sync with me as her legs tightly wrapped themselves around my waist. After a few more thrusts, I pulled out and turned her on her stomach, tracing her back with the soft strokes of my tongue. I could feel her body tremble as I buried myself deep inside her from behind. She came and now it was my turn. I amped up the pace, my heart rapidly beating and the sensation of a full explosion coming on. The sexual sounds that escaped her excited me as I couldn't hold back any longer. I pulled out and expelled everything I had onto the silky skin of her back. I was so caught up in the moment and the feeling, I had completely forgotten about a condom, and I was surprised she didn't say something to me about it.

I climbed off her and went into the bath for some tissue.

"Stay in my bed tonight," I spoke as I cleaned her back.

"Are you sure?" she asked.

"I'm positive." A small smile crossed my lips.

We both climbed under the sheets and I placed my arm around her while she snuggled against me and laid her head on my chest.

"You could have come inside me," she spoke. "I'm on birth control."

"You are?" I asked with surprise.

"Yes."

"Why didn't you say something before?"

"I don't know. You reached for a condom, so I thought you felt more comfortable using one."

"I've never not used one since Angelique, and I don't know why I didn't this time."

Chapter Thirty-Three

Zoey

That was really the first time he said her name to me. As I lay against him, I softly stroked his chest with my fingers. This felt right. Every time we had sex, it felt right. He was a different man, but the change I saw in him today and how a piece of the darkness that shrouded him lifted, I got my hopes up he was starting to see things differently.

"I think we should get some sleep," he spoke. "Good night, Zoey." He kissed the top of my head.

"Good night, Carter."

I opened my eyes and looked at the big red numbers on the clock that read two thirty a.m. As hard as I tried to go back to sleep, I couldn't. I carefully and quietly climbed out of bed, grabbed the white robe that was hanging on the hook in the bathroom, and sat out on the small balcony that housed two lounge chairs. I sat there, staring at the darkened water and listened as the waves crashed against the shoreline. I didn't know what was going to happen with us or if he could ever fully understand who I was. But he had to know I was falling in love with him and I couldn't stop it. Suddenly, a rush of cold settled inside me.

"You have to make him open up about me," I heard a voice whisper. "It's the only way he'll heal."

I looked over to my right and saw Angelique standing there.

"He needs you, Zoey."

Then she was gone.

"What are you doing out here?" Carter asked as he stepped onto the balcony.

"I couldn't sleep. I hope I didn't wake you."

"You didn't. I woke up and you were gone. Come back to bed."

I stared straight into the vast open water and ignored his request.

"When the plane crashed and I opened my eyes, I was standing in a field of flowers. The sun was so bright I could barely see. But I could feel love and peace all around me."

"What?" He took a seat in the chair next to me.

"A man and a woman walked over to me and each took my hand. We walked through the field of flowers together. The colors were so vibrant and the smell that filled the air was something I'd never smelled before. They explained to me that I was special and it wasn't my time to stay with them. They told me that I had a purpose and that purpose was to help those who were dying not to be afraid and tell them of my experience and what I saw. They said that I wasn't to be afraid of what awaited me on the other side and that two nice men were going to raise me and guide me along the way. I was to help those in need."

"What did they mean by 'what awaited you on the other side'?" he asked.

"After they sent me back and I woke up, Scott was there and picked me up. As he was carrying me off the plane, I watched all the souls of the people who died in the crash walk away, including my parents. But I didn't feel sad. I smiled and waved to them because I knew the place they were going to."

"Jesus, Zoey. I—"

"Every day since then, I am able to see the souls of those who passed, and some I have to help."

"What do you mean you have to help?"

"Sometimes, I have to give their loved ones a message before they can move on. Like the guy at the hotel. He needed me to tell his wife that everything she needed was locked in the safe in their bedroom and the combination was taped under the drawer of his nightstand."

"Have you ever told anyone else about this?" he asked.

"My dads know and my best friend, Holly. I knew I could trust her. We're soul sisters."

"I don't know what to think or what to say about any of it," he spoke with a shaky voice.

"You don't have to say anything, Carter. I just needed you to listen."

"I'm going to head back to bed. I think it would be a good idea if you slept in your room."

I swallowed hard as I felt the stabbing of a knife go through my heart.

"I will if that's what you really want," I sadly spoke.

"It is. I'm sorry."

He looked at me and then got up from his chair and went back inside. After a few moments, when I knew he was in bed, I went through the adjoining door, closed it, and climbed into my own bed. The truth was out and how he chose to deal with it had nothing to do with me. I couldn't make him accept it. That would be something he'd have to do on his own.

"Give him time," Nora whispered as she placed her hand on mine. "Eventually, he will accept it and he'll see things differently."

But I wasn't so sure about that.

The next morning around eight a.m., I climbed out of bed, showered, and got dressed. I didn't know if Carter was up and I wasn't about to find out, so I went down to the café in the hotel for a cup of coffee and a donut. As I was sitting there, I saw Carter approaching my table.

"I knocked on your door and you didn't answer. I also tried to call you, but I heard your phone ringing in your room," he spoke in a stern tone.

"Sorry, I just came down for a cup of coffee. How did you sleep?" I cautiously asked.

"How the hell do you think I slept after what you told me last night?"

"I'm sure you still have questions," I spoke.

"Actually, I don't. I've rented a boat and we'll be heading out in about an hour. I'm going back up to my room. I'll knock when it's time to leave." He turned and walked away.

I rolled my eyes and slowly shook my head. I could feel the tears emerging and I tried to stop them. After I finished my coffee and donut, I went back up to my room.

****

Carter

I lay on the bed with my hands behind my head still thinking about everything she told me last night. I didn't know what to think or even how to process any of it. All of it was crazy to me. I heard her door shut and I jumped off the bed because I needed to tell her something and I couldn't wait any longer. When I knocked on the adjoining door, she opened it.

"Are we leaving now?" she asked.

"No. There's something I need to tell you."

"What is it?"

"I'm going to Hawaii alone, so you'll need to book a flight home." I turned and began to walk away.

Suddenly, I felt a tight grip on my arm.

"Why?" Zoey shouted.

"Because I want to be alone!" I shouted back.

"Ah, of course you do because that's what you're good at. You're a perfectionist when it comes to pushing people away. If anyone says something you don't like or don't want to hear, you run the other way. I've seen you do it with Nora and with me!" she continued to shout.

"You don't know what the fuck you're talking about. We aren't good together and we never will be! Get that through your head! I'm not looking for a girlfriend or anyone to connect with. I'm happy living my life the way I do."

"Who said anything about wanting to be your girlfriend? I can't even stand you!" she shouted and caught me off guard.

I stood there and stared into her angry eyes.

"The only goddamn fucking reason I'm here is because they won't let me leave!" she angrily spewed.

I'd never heard her talk like that before and I was taken aback.

"Who won't let you leave?"

"Nora and Angelique! You think it was just a coincidence that my plane had mechanical problems and your rental car wouldn't start? You think us meeting in the airport was an accident? What about LaGuardia and JFK having power outages? What about my flight getting canceled and there only being one seat left on the flight here?! The one directly across from you! I'm supposed to finish this trip with you and they'll make sure it happens!"

"And why the fuck would they do that?" I angrily shouted at her.

"Because I'm supposed to help you! Damn it, Carter. Open your eyes and your mind. Leave your dark world for a minute and think about this."

"You're nuts! You fabricated that whole little story because you needed something to cling to because of the trauma from the plane crash!"

She stood there, a few feet from me, trembling from head to toe.

"Tell him to stay cool and not give Miss Harper a hard time anymore. Tell him that he was the best friend I ever had and he's going to be okay."

I swallowed hard and stood there, feeling paralyzed.

"What did you just say?"

She placed her hand on her head and turned away from me. I grabbed her arm and forced her to look at me.

"What did you just say?!"

"Let go of me." She tried to get out of my grip, but I wasn't letting her.

"Not until you answer my question!" I yelled through gritted teeth.

"Your friend, Andy. You were in an accident with him and his mom. He died and you broke your leg and needed surgery."

"How the fuck do you know that?"

"Because I was the little girl who was on the other side of the curtain. I was the one who spoke those very words to you that day."

My heart started to pound and I loosened my grip from her arm. Taking a seat on the bed, I rested my face in my hands as the memories of that day came flooding back. The little girl who came to my bedside. The feeling I felt when she placed her hand on mine. Those words. The ones Andy told her to tell me. I believed her then because there was no way she knew about my teacher, Miss Harper.

"Angelique told you that she loved you first, in the Empire State Building, about a month after you started seeing each other. You were having dinner and you reached across the table and knocked over her glass of red wine, spilling it all over the beige dress she was wearing. You felt so bad, and as you tried to clean the spots off her dress, she whispered that she loved you in your ear."

I looked up at her in disbelief.

"After she died, you were going through her things and you found the cuff links she had bought you as a gift for your birthday. You wrapped them in a black silk cloth and keep them hidden in a small black box on the top shelf of your bedroom closet."

"How the hell do you know that? I never told anyone about those cufflinks. Not even Nora."

"How do you think I know, Carter? I'll leave you alone now."

She turned and went back in her room, closing and locking the adjoining door behind her. I sat there for a moment and then fell back onto the bed, closing my eyes for a moment to get hold of myself, my thoughts, and my feelings.

Chapter Thirty-Four

Zoey

I didn't know what was going to happen and I wasn't going to sit around and wait. I was done being treated like I was nothing. His hot and cold personality made me want to rip my hair out. I tried. I gave everything I had and I was more than patient. Not only was I physically and mentally exhausted, I was hurt and broken. No one had ever made me feel this way and I didn't care if I ever saw Carter Grayson again. Wiping the tears that fell down my face, I grabbed my suitcase and headed to the airport. I was getting home one way or another.

I managed to get on the first flight back to New York. There were no hiccups and I landed safely. I took a cab to Carter's penthouse and called Sadie from the lobby to let her know I was there to pick up the rest of my things. As I stepped off the elevator, she greeted me with a hug.

"Why are you back already? And where's Mr. Grayson?"

"Mr. Grayson is still in Seattle or probably on his way to Hawaii. Who the hell knows and who the hell cares," I spoke as I walked to the bedroom to collect my things.

"You didn't kill him, did you?" She smirked.

"Unfortunately, no. Not that he didn't deserve it, though. We got into a huge fight and to be honest, Sadie, I don't ever want to see that man again."

"I'm sorry, Zoey. I had hoped you would have helped him."

"He can't be helped. I tried and I did everything I could. You can't save someone who doesn't want to be saved."

I gathered the rest of my things, hugged Sadie goodbye, and climbed into Holly's car that was waiting for me at the curb. The moment I shut the door, she reached over and hugged me as tears filled my eyes.

"I'm sorry, Zoey. He's an asshole and you need to forget about him. Put him out of your mind the best you can and go on with your life. You were fine before him and you'll be fine now."

"I know," I lied.

She pulled up in the driveway, and I took my suitcases from the back. After thanking her for picking me up and saying goodbye, I opened the door and stepped into my house. It felt good to be home again.

"Sweetheart." John stood in front of me with his arms out.

Setting my suitcases down, I cried in his arms. Scott walked over and wrapped his arms around both of us.

"Why don't you go upstairs, take a hot relaxing bath, and climb into bed. I made some homemade chicken noodle soup and I'll bring it up," Scott spoke.

I nodded my head, wiped my tears, and went upstairs. Climbing into the bubbly filled water, I lay back and closed my eyes.

****

Carter

I heard the door to her room shut. She was probably going down to get some coffee or something. I replayed everything she said over and over again in my head. Nothing that happened was a coincidence, and now I knew that. I said some horrible things to her. Things she didn't deserve to hear. But everything she said to me, I fully deserved. Zoey Benson was special. Not just to the world, but to me, and that was something I was ready to accept.

I got up from the bed and headed down to the lobby to find her. I checked the restaurants and the café, and when I couldn't find her, I went up to the lobby desk.

"May I help you?" an older gentleman asked.

"I'm looking for the woman who was with me. Tall, blonde, beautiful. Have you by any chance seen her?"

"I'm afraid I haven't, sir."

"Okay. Thank you."

I walked away, and as I was heading to the lobby door, one of the bellhops stopped me.

"Excuse me, Mr. Grayson?"

"Yes." I stopped.

"The woman who was with you, Zoey. She left."

"What do you mean she left?"

"I helped her with her suitcase. She got into a cab and headed to the airport."

I let out a long sigh.

"Thank you." I reached into my pocket and handed him a twenty-dollar bill.

There was no way she went home. She specifically told me they wouldn't let her. Pulling my phone from my pocket, I called the airport.

"Could you tell me if any flights to Connecticut or New York were canceled or delayed today?"

"All flights are leaving and arriving on time, sir. There haven't been any cancellations or delays to either of those places."

"Thank you."

I went back to my room and threw my phone on the bed.

"Really?" I threw my hands up and looked up at the ceiling. "After all this, you let her go?"

I shook my head and a rush of coldness flowed through me.

"I know you're here, Nora. I'm sorry. I'm sorry for everything and I'm going to make things right with her. I fucked up. I now know why you did what you did. Why you sent us on this trip to scatter your ashes. Why you wanted us together. You saw it and you knew that she was the one who could save me."

I sat down on the edge of the bed and placed my elbows on my knees.

"Maybe I knew it all along too and that's why I reacted the way I did. I felt the connection between us from the moment my eyes laid sight on her in Starbucks that day, and that's why I freaked out. I hadn't felt that in so long. But don't you worry, little sister, I'm going to fix this. And by the way, you're going to have to wait to have your ashes scattered in Hawaii because I'm not doing it alone."

I grabbed my phone and got up from the bed. I was late for the boat and I needed to get Nora's ashes out in Puget Sound before I headed back home to talk to Zoey.

I was on the boat, drifting in the open waters, when my phone rang.

"Cliff, what's up?" I answered.

"Good news, Carter. There are three offers on your Malibu beach house. Actually, all three clients are fighting over it. One client is offering a quarter million more than you're asking. Will you accept it?"

"No. In fact, take the house off the market. I've changed my mind. I'm not selling it after all."

"Are you sure?"

"Positive. Give my apologies to the buyers."

I ended the call, and as Nora's ashes scattered over the open water, I spoke, "Did you hear that, Nora? I'm not selling the beach house. There are too many good memories there and I'm not willing to give them up. The memories that we made there and that Angelique and I made were made out of love and I want to keep it and make new memories without forgetting the old ones. That house will stay in the Grayson family and memories will be made there for years to come."

I took the boat back in, called the pilot of my private jet that was flying me to Hawaii, and asked him to take me back to New York instead. As I sat on the plane, I knew I needed to devise a plan to see Zoey. It wasn't like I could just call her up and ask her to meet me. She hated me at the moment and there was no way she would come. I thought about going to her, but she'd probably just slam the door in my face.

When I arrived back at my penthouse, Sadie was waiting for me like I had asked.

"Welcome home, Mr. Grayson," she spoke.

"Thank you, Sadie. It's good to see you." I kissed her cheek.

"I can take your luggage up for you."

"No need. I can do it myself. I need your help."

"Okay. What would you like me to do?"

"I need you to call Zoey and tell her that she left a couple things here. Tell her they were in the dryer or something. I need her to come here so I can talk to her."

"Mr. Grayson, she doesn't want to talk to you ever again."

"Did she say that?"

"Yes." She looked down.

"Well, that's just too bad because she's going to listen to what I have to say. Now, when she comes to collect her things, I'll be here waiting for her."

"But she didn't leave anything behind," Sadie spoke.

"I know, and that doesn't matter. I just need you to get her in this penthouse. I'll take it from there. Go ahead, give her a call."

"But it's late and she'll wonder why I'm still here. I think it would be better to wait until the morning."

I sighed. "I suppose you're right. We don't want her to get suspicious. Fine, call her in the morning and let me know when she'll be stopping by. I'm heading to the office first thing."

"I will. Is that all?"

"Yes. Have a good night, Sadie."

"You as well, Mr. Grayson."

Chapter Thirty-Five

Zoey

After my bath, I climbed into bed and Scott brought up a tray with a bowl of chicken noodle soup and a roll on it.

"Here you go, sweetheart," he spoke as he set the tray over me and then gently kissed my forehead.

"We're happy you're home." John smiled.

Both of them took a seat on the edge of the bed.

"Do you remember a boy on the other side of the curtain from me that day of the plane crash?" I asked John. "He was in a bad car accident and broke his leg in three places and needed surgery?"

"Yeah. I think I do remember. He was the boy you were talking to when I came to get you and take you down for x-rays. Why?"

"That little boy was Carter Grayson."

"What?" He shook his head in disbelief.

"How do you know that for sure?" Scott asked.

"It came to me in a dream and I remembered. Now, twenty years later, I met him again."

"You were supposed to, sweetheart," John spoke. "We all know nothing happens by coincidence. This meeting had been lined up for twenty years. I believe you had to go through some things over the years before you were ready to meet him again and the same for him. The brief encounter in the hospital was just a taste of what the future held. You of all people know that. So don't try to deny it."

"I know he hurt you, Zoey. Your first heartbreak at twenty-five years old." Scott ran his finger down my cheek. "You never let anyone get really close to you because you knew they weren't the one you were meant to be with."

"I don't want to be with a man like him. He's horrible, and the things he said to me."

"Eat your soup and get some rest. You'll feel better about things in the morning," John spoke as he kissed my forehead.

I loved them both, but they were wrong. It would take me a long time to get over this.

****

The next morning, I climbed out of bed around noon and checked my phone. I noticed I had a missed call from Sadie.

"Hello," she answered.

"Hi, Sadie, it's Zoey. You called earlier?"

"Hi, Zoey. You left a couple of things here."

"I don't think so. I double checked before I left the penthouse."

"I found two of your shirts sitting on top of the dryer. You must have forgotten they were there."

"Oh. Okay. I'll head into the city tomorrow. There's a couple things I need to do. I'll call you before I come. He won't be there, right?"

"No. He's not back from his trip yet. So don't worry about that. It'll just be me here."

"Okay. Good. I'll call you tomorrow."

"See you then, sweetie."

That was odd. I didn't remember doing laundry before we left for California. Oh well, I wanted to go into the city anyway for the day and do some retail therapy. Today, I had an appointment with Holly to get my hair highlighted and trimmed.

****

Carter

I was sitting at my desk when a call from Sadie came in.

"Hello, Sadie. Did you talk to her?"

"I did, Mr. Grayson."

"And?"

"She's stopping by tomorrow."

"Tomorrow? Why not today?"

"I don't know. She said she was coming into the city tomorrow."

"What time?"

"She said she'll call before she stops by."

I sighed.

"Sadie, I need a time. Call her back. Make it tomorrow around six o'clock. Invite her to dinner or something."

"Mr. Grayson—"

"Sadie, this is important. Call me back and let me know what she says."

****

Zoey

I was sitting in the chair while Holly was putting the highlights in my hair when my phone rang.

"I have to answer this," I spoke to her.

"Sure, go ahead."

"Hello," I answered.

"Zoey, it's Sadie. I completely forgot. I have a bunch of errands to run tomorrow and a doctor's appointment. Can you come by around six? I'll make us a nice dinner."

"Yeah. Six will be fine. I'll just make the penthouse my last stop before I head home. We can actually meet somewhere for dinner if you'd like and you can just bring my things."

"Nope. I'm cooking for you. It's been a while. Plus, it'll be quieter here and it'll give us a chance to really talk."

"Okay, but I don't want you to go to any trouble."

"It's no trouble at all. I enjoy cooking for you. I'll see you around six o'clock tomorrow."

"See you then, Sadie."

"What was that all about?" Holly asked.

"I'm having dinner with Sadie tomorrow night at six."

"At Carter's penthouse?"

"Yeah. He's still away and Sadie sounds a little down. Plus, I left a couple of things there."

****

Carter

My phone rang and Sadie was calling.

"What did she say?" I answered.

"She's coming for dinner at six o'clock tomorrow."

"Excellent. I knew you could do it, Sadie. Did she sound suspicious or anything?"

"Not that I could tell."

"Okay. Good. Thanks again. You're a doll for doing this."

After ending the call, I immediately started to search flowers online. After our discussion at Pike Market Place, I needed to find the perfect flowers with the perfect meaning for her. Any old flower wouldn't do and I couldn't fuck this up. I needed her to see and believe how sorry I was.

Chapter Thirty-Six

Zoey

I headed into the city around one o'clock, grabbed some lunch, and did a lot of shopping. I didn't actually buy anything and I didn't know why. I think I just needed the distraction of looking around and being surrounded by people to make me forget about Carter. It was five thirty and I phoned Sadie to tell her I was stuck in horrible traffic and I might be a little late. As luck would have it, I arrived at the penthouse at precisely six o'clock. As the elevator doors opened, I stepped into the foyer and called out for Sadie.

"Sadie, I'm here," I spoke as I set my purse down on the table.

"Hello, Zoey," Carter spoke as he walked towards me with his hands tucked into his pants pockets.

My heart started racing and I broke out in a sweat.

"What are you doing here?" I asked.

"Well, considering this is where I live." He smirked.

"Sadie said you were still away." I grabbed my purse from the table.

"I had Sadie tell you that because I needed to talk to you, and I knew that if you knew I was here, you'd never come."

"I have nothing to say to you, and you're right, I wouldn't have come."

I pushed the button to the elevator. As soon as the doors opened, I began to step inside.

"I'll never forget the day Angelique told me she was pregnant with my child," he spoke. "It was the happiest day of my life."

I stood there for a moment, one foot in the elevator and one foot out.

"I was going to be a father. My life was complete. My business was growing, I had a woman that I loved, and a baby on the way."

I slowly removed my foot from the elevator and took a step back. The doors shut and I turned around and faced Carter.

"My life wasn't so great growing up. I lost my best friend, Andy, Nora got sick with cancer, my mother passed away, and then my father committed suicide. I had to drop out of college, take care of Nora, and try to save the company from bankruptcy. That company was all Nora and I had left in this world. Then I met Angelique, and suddenly, everything fell into place. I saw my future."

I just stood there, staring into his sad eyes, unable to speak.

"Please, come in and sit down. I'll pour us a glass of wine." He held out his hand to me.

When I placed my hand in his, he led me into the living room and over to the couch. He walked over to the bar and poured us each a glass of wine. Walking over to me, he handed me my glass and sat down next to me.

"The day I got the call about the accident, I was supposed to go to her doctor's appointment with her. The plan was that I was going to pick her up from work and we'd go together. But, I got tied up in a meeting. The client was being difficult and I couldn't leave. So, I sent her a text message and told her that I'd meet her there. If only I had told that client to fuck off and left the meeting when I was supposed to, she and my son would be alive."

I was too scared to say anything to him for the fear that he would get angry, because I knew he didn't want to hear what I had to say. I reached over and placed my hand on his.

"It's okay, Zoey. You can say it. After their death, I completely shut down. I hated this world, God, and my life. No one, and I mean no one, should ever have to experience so much death. I became angry and nothing mattered to me anymore except my company and Nora, of course. I secluded myself. I didn't grieve properly because every day I lived, I hoped that it was all a nightmare, and one day I'd wake up and she and my son would be next to me. I became bitter and secluded myself from everyone and everything. I lost friends because of it. They tried to help, but when they couldn't, they left. Nora did what she could, but I wouldn't listen to her. Then, she was diagnosed and the small narrow piece of the ledge I was standing on crumbled under me."

Tears filled my eyes as did his. My heart broke into tiny pieces listening to his story.

"I'm sorry, Zoey. I'm sorry for everything. For my behavior towards you and every horrible word I spoke to you."

"It's okay, Carter," I whispered.

"No. It's not okay and I need to explain to you why I did it. The moment I saw you in Starbucks, I felt something. Even though I didn't know you, I felt this strong connection or pull towards you. But I didn't think about it because I thought I'd never see you again. Then that night when you showed up here, I lost it. That's why I didn't want you here. Because I knew you were someone special and different. I resisted and did everything I could to keep my feelings buried. I've seen a lot of women since Angelique died. Actually, I used them and I'm ashamed of it. But, not one of those women ever touched me the way you have. When you started talking about seeing spirits and heaven and how everything happens for a reason, I forced myself not to believe in any of it because then it would be real and I didn't want to live in reality. I'm sorry for calling you crazy. I didn't mean it. I just wanted to convince myself that you were, even though I knew you weren't, because then it would be easy for me not to fall for you." He ran his hand down my cheek. "Even when we slept together, the connection was so deep. Deeper than what I had with Angelique and I felt guilty for that."

"Carter."

"How many times have you seen her? Please tell me. I want to know everything. I need to know."

"Quite a bit. I saw her here, but mostly at the beach house. She was with us the whole time. She's here, Carter, because you won't let her go and she can't move on until you do."

"And Nora?"

"Same thing. All she wants is for you to be okay. She loves you so much and it hurt her to see you living the way you are. Her illness wasn't her focus, you were. You were all she worried about."

"Of course she did. She always worried about everyone else. Zoey, have you seen my son?"

A tear streamed down my face as I lightly nodded my head.

"He looks just like you. He's beautiful."

Tears started to run down his face.

"We were meant to meet that day in the hospital. I know now that wasn't a coincidence," he spoke.

"No, it wasn't. And we had to go through everything we did over the past twenty years in order to meet each other again."

"The man you met a few months ago isn't who I am."

"I know." I brought my hand up to his face and wiped away his tears.

"You were right when you told me I became a victim of circumstance. I didn't know any other way to deal with everything. I felt like I didn't deserve to be happy."

"You do deserve to be happy, Carter. Everyone deserves happiness. No matter what. That's all Angelique and Nora want for you. They want you to live again and find happiness. Isn't that what you'd want for them if the situation was reversed?"

"Of course I would."

"Then why would you think they wouldn't want the same for you?"

"I don't know. I was lost, so lost that I couldn't find my way back. But you found me. You, Zoey, and you brought me back. You opened my eyes again."

He leaned over and wrapped his arms around me, pulling me into him.

"I know there aren't enough words in the world for me to say to you. But I will tell you that I miss you and I'm sorry. I wouldn't blame you if you didn't forgive me. Hell, I wouldn't forgive me."

"I do forgive you, Carter."

"You do?" He broke our embrace and looked into my eyes.

"Yes." I smiled. "I missed you too."

"How did you get home? I mean, I know you flew home, but I thought Nora and Angelique would have stopped you."

"I think they realized you needed some time alone to process everything."

"I felt Nora in the hotel room when I was talking to her. A coldness rushed through me."

"She was there at the Grand Canyon and she did place her hand on your shoulder. I'm sorry I lied to you about it. I just didn't want you to get angry again."

"I knew she was there. And at times, when I'm alone at night in my office, I swear I can feel Angelique's presence."

"That's because you did. She was there with you."

Chapter Thirty-Seven

Zoey

We sat on the couch, locked in an embrace for several minutes while Carter stroked my hair and held me tight.

"I have something for you," he spoke.

"You do?"

"I'll be right back." He smiled as he kissed my head.

A moment later, he walked over to me with his hand behind his back.

"These are for you."

I smiled as I took the beautiful bouquet of white flowers from him and brought them up to my nose.

"Star of Bethlehem." I grinned. "Where on earth did you get these? They're very hard to find."

"It was tricky." He winked. "Do you know what they symbolize?"

"They're an 'I'm sorry' flower."

"Not only that, but they also represent a redo and ask for a chance to right a wrong. That's what I'm asking you for, Zoey.

Give me another chance. Let me make right everything I've done wrong. When I told you back in Seattle that we weren't good together, I was lying. I know deep down in my heart, we can be amazing together. That's if you'll let me show you."

As I sat there and stared at him, I couldn't help but smile. He was so handsome and every last bit of darkness that he had been shrouded in for the past five years had disappeared. I stood up and wrapped my arms around his neck, brushing my lips softly against his.

"You don't have to show me. I already know we will be."

He let out a breath.

"Thank you." He hugged me tight and I closed my eyes.

A moment later, I opened them, and standing in front of me were Angelique and Nora, holding hands and smiling.

"They're here," I whispered in his ear.

"Where?" he asked as he broke our embrace.

"Behind you. Umm, you didn't go to Hawaii?" I asked.

"Oh. Well, no. I already apologized to Nora about that and told her I wasn't going alone. So you need to repack because we're going to Hawaii together, like planned, to scatter the last of her ashes." He smirked.

"That won't be a problem because I haven't even unpacked yet." I laughed.

"Let's drive to your house and pick up your suitcase. You can spend the night here and we'll leave tomorrow. I have the private jet on standby. Wait, Sadie made dinner. Why don't you call John and Scott and have them come over for dinner? That way, they can bring your suitcase and I can get to know them better."

"Sounds like fun. I'll call them right now."

I went to the foyer, grabbed my phone from my purse, and called my dad, John, who was happy to hear what I told him.

"He said he and Scott will be here within the hour." I smiled as I walked over to Carter.

He reached down and scooped me up in his arms.

"Good. That gives me just enough time to make love to you." He grinned.

****

Carter

I hired a tour guide to take Zoey and me to Sweetheart Rock to scatter the last of Nora's ashes.

"I'm a little surprised as to why your sister would want her ashes scattered here, Mr. Grayson," Ano, our guide spoke.

"Why?"

"You've never heard the legend?"

"No. I can't say that I have."

"I haven't either," Zoey spoke.

"It's a story about a warrior and the beautiful princess he was going to marry. The warrior was so in love with his princess that he was afraid other men would be taken by her beauty, so he hid her away in that sea cave right over there." He pointed. "Then one day, a Kona storm came through and the princess drowned. The warrior took her body and buried her where the top of that rock is over there. Because he was so heartbroken and grief stricken, he took his own life by jumping from the top of the rock."

"Wow," Zoey spoke. "How tragic."

"I'll leave the two of you alone for a while. When you're ready to head back, just let me know."

"Thank you, Ano," I spoke and then glanced over at Zoey. "You don't by any chance see the warrior and his princess around here, do you?"

"No." She laughed.

"I now know why Nora wanted her ashes scattered here."

"Why?" Zoey asked.

"Because of my father. He was so heartbroken after my mother died."

She placed her arm around me and laid her head on my shoulder.

"I'm sorry, Carter."

"Let's get these ashes scattered. Shall we?"

I took off my shirt and Zoey slipped out of her shorts and tank top that was covering up her bathing suit. I grabbed her hand and we walked into the water. It wasn't possible to swim to the rock, so I turned the box over and let her ashes out into the water. We stood there and watched them drift away from us and towards the rock.

"She's here," Zoey spoke. "She's standing on top of the rock."

"I really hate that I can't see her."

"Close your eyes, Carter. You'll feel her presence."

"Goodbye, Nora. May you rest in peace," I spoke.

We got out of the water, grabbed our towels, and laid them down in the sand. I glanced over at Zoey and pushed a strand of hair behind her ear while I smiled at her.

"What?" She smiled back.

"Is it too early in our relationship to tell you that I'm in love with you?"

"I don't think so."

"I won't scare you off or anything?"

"I don't know. Maybe you should try telling me and see what happens."

"I love you, Zoey." I ran my fingers through her hair.

"I love you too, Carter." She brought her hand up to my face.

My smile widened as I leaned in and softly brushed my lips against hers.

Chapter Thirty-Eight

Zoey

Carter and I spent two full weeks in Hawaii. We didn't plan on staying that long, but we were having so much fun, we decided to stay. We went from island to island, stayed at various high-end hotels, went on an open-door volcano helicopter ride, swam with the dolphins, went snorkeling, visited some art galleries and museums, went on a sunset dinner cruise, attempted to surf, shopped, and spent quality time on the beautiful beaches. But nothing was better than all the sex we had. It was the trip of a lifetime and I had never been so happy.

It was our last morning in Hawaii and we were lying in bed, our bodies snuggled against each other's.

"I'm thinking about moving," he spoke.

I lifted my head from his chest and looked at him.

"What? Why?"

"I think it's time for a change. A new start in a new place." He smiled.

"Where are you moving to?"

"Same area. Different building. I have options."

"You mean you have buildings you already own." I grinned.

"That too." He smirked. "There's only one problem."

"What?"

"I want someone to move in with me, but I'm not sure if she wants to."

"Well, the only way you'll find out is if you ask that someone."

"And what if she says no?"

"What if she says yes?" I smiled.

"Okay, here it goes. Will you move in with me, Zoey?"

"Yes. I would love to move in with you, Carter."

A wide grin crossed his lips.

"Do you know how happy that makes me that you said yes?"

"Do you know how happy that makes me that you asked?"

"I guess we're just two happy people, aren't we?" He grinned.

"Yes, we are."

He rolled me over on my back and hovered over me.

"I love you," he spoke.

"I love you too."

****

Two Weeks Later

When Carter Grayson decided he wanted something, he didn't wait. The minute we landed in New York, he took me over to look at the penthouse we'd be living in. Needless to say, I fell in love with it the moment I stepped inside the six-bedroom, six-bathroom beauty. Because he decided to sell his other penthouse fully furnished, we spent the last two weeks shopping every day for furniture for every room in the house.

While the moving company was at our new home unpacking all the kitchen stuff and putting it away, Sadie kept a very close eye on them, directing them to where she wanted everything to go. I could hear my phone ringing from the other room, and when I picked it up, I saw it was Holly calling.

"Hello."

"What are you doing right now?"

"Just getting settled into the new penthouse. What are you doing?"

"Standing at your elevator waiting to come up."

"Oh my God! Come up! I can't wait for you to see it."

I stood in front of the elevator doors, and when they opened, I gave Holly a big hug. I hadn't seen her in a while with all the craziness.

"What the hell, Zoey? This is gorgeous!" she spoke as she looked around.

I gave her the grand tour and Sadie made us each a cup of coffee. Taking it over to the couch, we sat down.

"I've missed you so much." I smiled at her.

"I've missed you too. I have some great news to tell you."

"What?"

"I'm moving to the city and I'm opening up my own hair salon and spa!" she screeched with excitement.

I bounced up and down on the couch as I reached over and hugged her.

"Where are you moving and where is your shop going to be?"

"Well." She grinned. "The shop is located at East 34th Street and I'm moving into this building in an apartment on the fourth floor! I've been in cahoots with your amazing boyfriend. He happens to own the building over on East 34th and he's giving me a super low rent deal on an apartment here. I take back every bad thing I ever said about him." She laughed.

"What? When did this happen?"

About a week ago. I ran into him on the street, we got to talking, and he made it happen."

"That's right. I remember him telling me he ran into you. But he didn't tell me about anything else."

"That's because I wanted it to be a surprise, sweetheart." Carter grinned as he walked over and kissed me. "Hello, Holly."

"Hey, Carter."

"Carter, thank you." I stood up and hugged him.

"The two of you are soul sisters and you shouldn't be living far apart. Plus, Holly told me she wanted to open her own shop one day and I just happened to have the perfect building. You can properly thank me later." He winked before kissing my lips. "Now, if you'll excuse me, I need to make sure my office here is set up."

"I can't believe the change in him," Holly spoke. "You did real good, Zoey."

"I believe it. He just needed to accept a few things." I smiled.

Chapter Thirty-Nine

Carter

We lay in bed, wrapped in each other's arms after making passionate love on our first night in our new home in our new bed. A bed that I would only ever share with her. Something had been gnawing at me for the past couple of weeks and I didn't know how to approach her about it. But, I just decided I needed to get it over with.

"There's something we need to talk about, Zoey. Something that's been on my mind for a while."

She lifted her head from my chest and stared up at me.

"What is it? It sounds serious."

I took in a deep breath.

"Have you given any thought about your job? I mean, I know you've taken a lot of time off since everything that's happened, and now that we're settled in here, I just was wondering what you're going to do. I'm not thrilled with you having to leave and live somewhere else while you take care of your patients."

"I know." She pressed her lips against my chest. "I'd been thinking about that also. I love my job, but things are different now. I still want to be a hospice nurse, so I'm going to have to figure things out. Meanwhile, I have enough money saved that I can take off some more time to figure it out."

"Money will never be an issue for you again. So, don't worry about that. I have all the money you need."

"Thank you, my love. But I would like to earn my own money."

"I understand that. You are a very independent woman." I kissed her head.

I silently let out a sigh of relief. She was on the same page I was and I couldn't be happier. While she was figuring out what she wanted to do, I was working out an idea in my head. But I didn't want to mention it to her until I planned to put things in motion.

****

Three Weeks Later

"It's good to see you so happy again, Carter," Ross spoke as he sat across from me.

"Thanks, man. I am happy and it feels really good."

"How's that deal coming along?"

"It's done. I got the call this morning. I can't wait to run it by Zoey."

"And what if she's not too keen about it?"

"I think she will be. But if she isn't, then I'll sell the building."

"You'll take a huge loss. You paid a pretty penny for that."

"I'm not worried about it. If I take a loss, I take a loss. I'm pretty confident that everything will work out. In fact, I'm going to pick up the keys now and then I'm going to call Zoey."

****

Zoey

I was helping Holly at her new shop when my phone rang.

"Hey, baby," I answered.

"Hello, gorgeous. What are doing right now?"

"Helping Holly at the shop. What are you doing?"

"Hoping you'll meet me somewhere. Is there any way you can escape for a while?"

"Sure. Where do you want to meet?"

"854 Fifth Avenue. Just let me know when you're on your way."

"I can meet you there in about fifteen minutes. May I ask why we're meeting there?"

"You'll see when you get here. I love you, darling."

"I love you too. See you soon."

"I sure hope that was Carter you were talking to." Holly smirked.

"Of course it was." I laughed. "I have to meet him at 854 Fifth Avenue, so I'm going to take off. I can come back after?"

"Nah. That's okay. I'm doing interviews for the rest of the afternoon. Go meet your man and have some fun."

When I walked out of Holly's shop, I saw Juan standing in front of the car.

"Hello, Zoey. Mr. Grayson sent me to get you."

"I just got off the phone with him. How did you get here so fast?" I asked as I climbed in the back.

"I was just around the corner having lunch."

Juan pulled up to the curb of 854 Fifth Avenue and I saw Carter standing there waiting for me. He walked over and opened the door.

"Hello, love." He smiled as he kissed my lips.

"Hi. What are we doing here?" I asked as I stared at the mansion before me.

"Come inside. I want you to see it." He took my hand.

"Carter, you're not thinking about moving again, are you? Because—"

He let out a chuckle. "No. We are not moving again. I'll explain everything once we step inside."

"Wow. Wow. Wow. This is gorgeous. On second thought, if you really wanted to move…" I grinned at him.

"First of all, this place is way too big, and second of all, Sadie would quit. Anyway, this is something I've been working on since we had our talk about your job three weeks ago."

"I don't understand."

"I bought this building with the hopes of turning it into a hospice care home."

"What?" I turned and looked at him with a shocked expression.

He placed his hands on my shoulders, and with a smile, he spoke, "Listen, sweetheart, I know how much your job means to you, so I want to turn this into a hospice care home and I want you to run it. In fact, the whole thing is yours."

I placed my hand over my mouth in disbelief. "Carter, oh my God, I can't believe you did this."

"Did I do a bad thing?" He cocked his head.

"No." I smiled as I reached up and kissed him. "You did a wonderful thing." Tears began streaming down my face.

"Why are you crying, sweetheart?"

"I'm just so happy."

He wrapped his arms around me and pulled me into an embrace.

"So it's a yes?" he asked.

"Yes. It's a yes! Thank you so much."

"Excellent." He smiled. "Come on, I'll show you around. It has fifteen bedrooms and three elevators, so we don't have to worry about the stairs for the patients. The one thing we will need to do is put a ramp outside, which won't be an issue. We can go over all the other details later. I just wanted you to see it first and hopefully approve of it."

"Of course I approve of it. But if I'm going to run this place, I'm going to need a partner or someone to help me run it."

"I have someone in mind." He winked. "You know what the best part of this place is?"

"What?" I asked.

"It's only four minutes from home. So, if an emergency arises, you'll be close by."

"Carter, I love you so much." I threw my arms around him.

"I know you do and I love you so much." He brushed his lips against mine. "By the way, we're having dinner with your dads tonight at Per Se at seven o'clock."

"Why do you know this and I don't?" I arched my brow at him.

"Because I'm the one who called and invited them." He grinned.

Chapter Forty

Zoey

With Carter's help and connections, we started renovating the twenty-thousand-square-foot mansion. It would be at least six to nine months before it was completed and then we'd be ready to open the doors. Two exciting things happened that night Carter and I met with my dads for dinner. The first thing was, they were moving to the city in the same building as me and Carter. They bought a beautiful two-bedroom apartment on the tenth floor. Of course, it was Carter's idea and he gave them a deal they couldn't refuse. My dad John quit his job at the hospital in Connecticut when Presbyterian Hospital offered him a full-time position he couldn't refuse. My dad Scott decided to retire as a fireman and offered to come and help me run the hospice center. He was the person Carter had in mind and had previously spoken to him about it after learning that he wanted to retire.

It was a Saturday night and Carter and I were getting ready to head to the Christmas party he was throwing for his staff at The Plaza Hotel.

"Damn, look at you," Carter spoke as he licked his lips.

"You like?" I asked as I did a twirl in the middle of the bedroom.

"What do you think?" He grinned as he looked down at his rising cock.

I smiled and patted him on his chest.

"You'll have to wait until after the party. We're already running late."

"I'm the boss. I can be as late as I want." He pulled me into him.

"It's not polite to keep your guests waiting." I pressed my lips against his.

"Have you by any chance seen my cuff links?"

"Aren't they in the jewelry box?" I asked.

"No. I looked already."

Suddenly, we heard something fall in the closet.

"What was that?" he asked as he walked over to the closet and opened the double doors.

He walked inside, bent down, and picked up the small black box with the cuff links in it that Angelique had bought him for his birthday.

"Where did these come from?" he asked me. "I thought I got rid of them."

"You did and I retrieved them." I lightly smiled. "There was no reason for you not to keep them. And obviously, she wants you to wear them tonight." I straightened his bow tie.

"Zoey, I—I've never worn them."

"Then tonight's as good a night as any to wear them for the first time. She bought these for you and never had the chance to give you them. She wants you to wear them, Carter."

"Is she here?"

"Not now. But, obviously, she was."

I took the cuff links out of the box and put them on him.

"There. Go look in the mirror."

He walked over to the full-length mirror and stared at them.

"Thank you." He turned to me with a smile.

"You're welcome."

He walked over to me and wrapped his arms around my waist.

"Have I told you lately how much I love you?"

"You have. But I want to hear it again."

"I love you to the moon and back, sweetheart," he spoke as his bright and happy eyes burned into mine.

"I love you too, Carter." He was so sexy and I couldn't get enough of him. "Fuck it, we can be late." I pushed him down on the bed and climbed on top of him.

****

Carter

It was Christmas morning and Zoey and I sat by our beautifully lit and decorated tree and exchanged gifts.

"Carter, I love it!" She hugged me after opening the new Chanel handbag I bought her.

She handed me a gift with a wide grin across her face. I took the wrapping off and removed the lid to the box, taking out the framed picture of the two of us that Ano took at Sweetheart Rock in Hawaii.

"I love this, Zoey. Thank you. This will be perfect on my desk."

"It's a special picture, Carter."

"I know. It's of the two of us." I grinned.

"No. Not just because of that. Look. See the white outlined figure on the rock? That's Nora."

Tears started to fill my eyes as I stared at it and then looked up at her.

"Merry Christmas, Carter," Zoey spoke.

"Thank you, sweetheart. Thank you for this. Merry Christmas. I love you so much."

"I love you too."

We finished opening the rest of our gifts, made love in the shower, and got dressed before her family and Holly arrived for dinner. I nervously paced back as I waited because I had one last gift for her.

"Zoey, are you almost ready?" I yelled.

"Yes. I'm ready. Why? They won't be here for at least another hour."

"I have one more gift for you," I spoke.

"You do?"

"Yes. I have to go get it, so stay right here and don't move."

"Okay." She smiled.

I went into the laundry room where I had a bouquet of purple roses hidden since yesterday. Grabbing them, I walked into the living room where she stood and handed them to her.

"Oh, Carter. They're gorgeous."

"You told me that the purple rose symbolizes soul mates, but it also symbolizes love at first sight." I inhaled a deep breath, took the flowers from her, set them down, and grabbed her left hand. "Zoey, I already told you that I felt this incredible connection to you when I first saw you in Starbucks, and every day, that connection grew stronger and stronger. I was so broken and lost at that time that I couldn't see what was in front of me. You stood by me even when I put you through hell and I will never forget that. My world was so dark and then you walked into it and you pushed all the darkness away."

"Carter." Tears filled her eyes.

"Shh. Let me finish, sweetheart. You took all my broken pieces, and when I thought it wasn't possible, you put me back together again. You made me whole, Zoey. I was imprisoned in my own personal hell and you set me free. You showed me what it was like to live again and I love you so much for that." I reached into my pocket and pulled out a small blue velvet box. Flipping open the top, I held it up in front of her. "You are my soulmate, the love of my life, my queen, and the person I was born to be with for the rest of my life. Will you marry me and become Mrs. Carter Grayson?"

She placed her right hand over her mouth as the stream of tears ran down her face.

"Yes, Carter. I will marry you!"

With a smile, I took the three-carat cushion-cut square diamond with a band of diamonds on each side from the box and slipped it on her finger. Then I brought my hand up to her face and wiped away her tears.

"I didn't mean for you to cry," I spoke with tears in my eyes.

"How could I not? You're so romantic and you make me happy, Carter. I love you so much."

"You make me the happiest man alive, sweetheart, and I love you."

Chapter Forty-One

Zoey

I couldn't stop staring at the gorgeous ring that sat on my finger. The moment John, Scott, and Holly walked in, I shamelessly showed it off. But they already knew about it. Carter had asked all three of them for their permission to take my hand in marriage. John and Scott openly welcomed him to the family and called him the perfect gentleman.

****

Nine Months Later

I took in a deep breath as my dads walked into the bridal room of the church.

"Wow," they both spoke at the same time with tears in their eyes.

"No." I waved my finger at them. "No tears. Not yet anyway."

"You look absolutely beautiful, baby." John kissed my cheek.

"You sure do. We always knew this day would come." Scott began to cry. "Sorry, I can't help it." He wiped his tears.

"Are you ready?" John asked as both he and Scott held out their arms.

"Yes. As ready as I'll ever be."

The music started to play and they slowly walked me down the aisle. The only thing I could see was my handsome husband-to-be standing nervously at the altar.

"Who gives this woman's hand in marriage?" the priest asked.

"We do," both John and Scott spoke at the same time.

After kissing my cheek, they placed my hand in Carter's.

"Are you okay?" I whispered to him.

"I've never been better. You?"

"Same." I smiled.

We said our vows, which had both of us crying along with all of our guests. And then we were pronounced Mr. and Mrs. Carter Grayson.

"You may kiss your bride, Carter." The priest smiled.

"It would be my pleasure."

After the ceremony and pictures, we headed to The Plaza Hotel for our wedding reception. We walked around, greeted our guests and had a wonderful dinner. It was time to share our first dance as husband and wife, and we danced to the song *How Long Will I Love You* by Ellie Goulding.

"You are so beautiful," he spoke as he smiled at me.

"So are you."

As we were dancing, I smiled as I stared at Nora and Angelique, who were a few feet away from us. When the song ended, the DJ announced he had a request for another song for us and not to leave the dance floor. My heart started racing because I had a feeling I knew what it was. Suddenly, *Unchained Melody* started to play. I looked at Carter, who swallowed hard.

"It's okay, Carter. She wants us to dance to this."

"She's here, isn't she?"

"Yes, and so is Nora."

"Tell her I said thank you." He smiled as we slowly danced.

****

Three Months Later

Carter and I spent a three-week honeymoon traveling around Europe and taking in the beautiful sights of Rome, the Amalfi Coast, Paris, and London. Once we got home, our lives went back to normal. Carter went back to running his company and I went back to the hospice center. So needless to say, our lives were pretty busy.

One morning after Carter left for the office and I was getting ready to work, Holly came over before she had to open the shop. I was standing in the bathroom doing my makeup when she walked in. Suddenly, the smell of her perfume sent a wave of nausea over me.

"What kind of perfume are you wearing?" I asked.

"The same kind I wear every day. Why?"

Placing my hand over my mouth, I ran over to the toilet and vomited.

"Oh my God, are you okay?" she asked as she held my hair back.

"I don't know. The smell of your perfume made me sick." I began to laugh. "I've been feeling a little sick to my stomach the last few days. I think I have a touch of the flu."

"Or a touch of a pregnancy." She smiled.

"Don't be ridiculous. I'm not pregnant." I wiped my mouth and stood up.

"Yeah. I think you are, Zoey." She grinned.

"I can't be. I'm on birth control. I get the shot every three mon—Oh my God, I forgot to get it last month! With everything going on and the hospice center, I forgot! And come to think of it, I never got my period last month."

"Yippee!" She jumped up and down. "I'm going to be an aunt!"

"Holly, we don't know for sure if I am."

"Well, the only way to find out is to go buy a pregnancy test and take it."

"I guess I'll have to." I bit down on my bottom lip.

"Okay. Call me when you take it and let me know. I have to go open the shop. I love you."

"I love you too. Have a good day."

I took a seat on the edge of the bed and pondered the thought that I might be pregnant. Carter and I never really discussed kids. I mean, we both wanted them, but we didn't talk about when. On my way to the hospice center, I stopped at the drug store and bought three different pregnancy tests. Going into the bathroom once I got to work, I peed on each stick and tried to wait patiently for the results, but I didn't have to, because instantly, the sticks turned positive. I was in shock, but a good shock. Carter and I were going to have a baby and I couldn't wait to tell him.

Since his birthday was only a week away, I kept the news to myself. As torturous as it was, I wanted it to be the best birthday ever for him.

"Happy birthday, baby." I smiled as I gently kissed his lips.

With his eyes still shut, he smiled.

"Thank you."

He opened his eyes and softly stroked my hair as I leaned over him. Rolling over, I pulled two gift bags out from under the bed.

"Open this one first." I grinned as I handed him the bag with the new watch he wanted.

"You didn't!" he exclaimed as he took it out of the bag and opened the box.

"I did." I smiled.

"How? They didn't have any left and weren't getting another shipment in for a couple of months."

"I had the salesman tell you that." I winked.

"Come here." He pulled me into him. "I love you. Thank you."

"I love you, and you have one more present to open."

"Sweetheart, the watch was more than enough."

"I think you'll like this better than the watch."

I handed him the bag, and after pulling the tissue paper from it, he took out a newborn white baby sleeper with little yellow ducks on it. He held it up and then looked at me.

"Does this mean—"

"Yes!" I nodded my head with excitement. "We're having a baby."

"We're having a baby? Me and you?" he asked in shock.

"Of course me and you!" I laughed.

"You're pregnant?"

"Oh my God, Carter, yes, I'm pregnant!"

"Zoey." He choked up. He brought his hand up to my cheek with tears in his eyes. "We're having a baby," he whispered.

I leaned in and brushed my lips against his as he wrapped me tightly in his arms. Then suddenly, he let go of me, jumped out of bed, opened the bedroom window, and yelled, "We're having a baby!"

Chapter Forty-Two

Carter

As the months flew by, I made sure to keep Zoey and the baby safe at all times. I could tell she was irritated by it, but she knew I was only doing it out of love. Today was the day we would find out the sex of our child at a gender reveal party that Holly was throwing us at our penthouse. It didn't matter to either one of us what the gender was. We just wanted him or her to be healthy.

Our friends gathered for dinner and drinks as we anxiously waited to cut the cake Holly had specially made for us.

"Okay, you two. It's time to find out the sex of your little one. I feel so special since I'm the only one who knows." She smirked.

"Holly, can we please get on with it?" I asked.

She laughed and handed Zoey the knife.

"Carter, put your hand on Zoey's, like you did when you cut your wedding cake. If the cake inside is blue, it's a boy; if it's pink, it's a girl. I'll count to three. One...two...three."

Zoey and I cut into the cake and took out a piece.

"We're having a girl!" Zoey exclaimed.

"Perfect." I kissed her lips with a grin across my face.

Everyone clapped and hugged us and we all enjoyed a piece of cake and toasted to the news.

A daughter. A little princess. I felt like I was living a dream and I never wanted to wake up. Later that evening, after everyone left, Zoey and I climbed into a warm bath, her back tightly pressed against my chest as my hands softly rubbed her growing belly.

"I love the idea of having a little princess running around here," I spoke.

"You're going to spoil her." Zoey smiled as she looked up at me.

"You bet I am. She's going to deserve the world, just like her mommy does." I kissed her head.

"You better be careful or you'll turn her into a little diva."

Suddenly, I felt her kicking my hand.

"Did you feel that, Zoey?" I asked in excitement.

"How could I not, Carter?" She laughed.

After our bath, Zoey climbed into bed with a book and I grabbed a pair of headphones from my nightstand and put them over her belly.

"What are you doing?" she asked as she arched her brow.

"Playing some music for the baby."

"What kind of music?"

"Just a song. No big deal."

Zoey took the headphones off her belly and brought them up to her ears.

"'Daddy's Little Girl'?" She laughed. "What are you doing? Brainwashing her?"

Taking the headphones from her, I placed them back on her belly.

"No. Of course not. How could you say such a thing? I just want her to know right now that she's daddy's little girl and I will always be there for her to love and protect her."

A tender smile crossed Zoey's lips as she brought her hand up to my cheek.

"You are an amazing daddy already."

****

We stood in the middle of the rose gold and white nursery that was now ready and waiting for our daughter. She was expected to arrive in two weeks and I couldn't wait to hold her.

"Everything looks perfect." Zoey smiled. "You did a great job, Carter."

"Thanks, sweetheart, but *we* did a great job. I can't believe how fast time is flying by."

"It may have flown for you, but for me, it feels like eternity." She smiled.

"Well, everything is done and put in its place, so now we just can sit back and wait."

"Umm. I don't think we have to. My water just broke." She looked down.

Chapter Forty-Three

Zoey

"What?!" Carter exclaimed. "You're not due for another two weeks."

"Tell that to your daughter, because obviously, she wants to be born now."

"Okay, don't panic, sweetheart. We got this."

"I'm not panicking, Carter."

"Are you in pain? What do you need me to do?"

"I'm not in any pain." I placed my hand on his chest. "You go get the bag we packed for the hospital and I will call Dr. Perry," I calmly spoke.

"Okay. Don't move. I'll be right back." He kissed my head.

He was so cute and nervous as hell. I placed my hands on my belly.

"Thank you, baby girl. I'll see you soon."

I picked up my phone, which was sitting on the dresser, and called Dr. Perry. He told me to go right to the hospital and he'd see me when I got there.

"I have your bag. Did you call Dr. Perry?" Carter asked.

"Yes. He said to come right to the hospital."

"Are you sure you're not in pain?" He lightly took hold of my arm as we walked out of the nursery.

"I'm positive, Carter. Trust me, you're going to know when I'm in pain."

We slowly walked down the stairs and took the elevator to the lobby. Juan had the night off, so we took a cab to the hospital.

"Can you please call my dads and Holly once we get there?" I asked as I laid my head on his shoulder.

"I already sent them a group text message, sweetheart." He took hold of my hand and brought it up to his lips.

We arrived at the Emergency room and Carter climbed out of the cab and grabbed a wheelchair for me. It just so happened that John was working and he met us outside.

"So, I hear your water broke." He smiled as he and Carter helped me into the wheelchair. "Are you having any contractions?"

"Not yet."

He wheeled me up to the labor and delivery unit where Dr. Perry was standing at the nurses' station. Giving me a kiss on my head, John spoke, "I have to get back downstairs, but I'll be up later to check on you."

"Thanks, Dad." I smiled.

Dr. Perry had a nurse wheel me into a private room, where I changed into a gown, lay down on the bed, and was hooked up to a fetal monitor.

"I can't believe this is happening already," Carter spoke as he took hold of my hand. "I don't want you to be nervous, sweetheart."

"I think you're more nervous than I am." I grinned at him.

"Okay. Let's see what's going on down there," Dr. Perry spoke as he examined me. "You are dilated to one centimeter. If contractions don't start within twelve hours, we're going to have to induce labor. Hopefully, we won't, but I'm just letting you know it's a possibility."

"How long could this take?" Carter asked him.

"It depends. Possibly twenty-four hours, but we'll do everything we can to make Zoey as comfortable as possible."

"No drugs," I spoke. "I'm doing this naturally."

"Okay. I will make a note of that in your chart. Meanwhile, I have two other women who are in labor now, but your nurse, Jessie, will keep me updated."

As soon as Holly and Scott arrived, Carter left the room for a while.

"I'm going to run downstairs for some coffee. I'll be right back, sweetheart." He leaned down and kissed my lips.

When he returned, he was holding two dozen roses with a smile on his face.

"Carter, they're beautiful."

"The red ones are for you and the pink ones are for our little girl."

It was getting late, so Holly left to go home and Scott went downstairs to see John.

"Why don't you try to get some sleep?" Carter spoke. "You have a long road ahead of you and you're going to need all the strength you can get."

"I am tired." I sleepily closed my eyes.

I don't think I was asleep even an hour, when suddenly, a rip-roaring pain shot through me.

"Holy shit!" I opened my eyes and yelled.

Carter jumped, for he was asleep in the chair.

"What? What's wrong!"

"I think I just had a contraction."

"Shit. Okay. I'll go get the nurse."

A moment later, Carter and Jessie walked into the room. She walked over to the baby monitor and glanced at the paper that was spewing out of it.

"Yes, Zoey. You definitely had a contraction. That's good news." She smiled. "You are officially in labor. I'm going to check you to see if you've dilated any more. Yep, you sure have. You're now at three centimeters. I'll go let Dr. Perry know."

After she walked out of the room, I looked at Carter, who was standing over me, gently rubbing my forehead with his thumb.

"Hopefully, it won't be too much longer." He smiled.

"I still have to get to ten centimeters." I narrowed my eye at him.

Another contraction emerged and I let out a screeching howl. This went on for four more hours.

"I can't do this anymore, Carter."

"Yes, you can, Zoey. You're one of the strongest people I know." He smiled. "I'm not leaving your side, not for one second. We're doing this together."

"NO WE'RE NOT!" I shouted as another contraction came. "I'm doing all the work. I'm the one in excruciating pain. You're standing there doing nothing!"

"Zoey, breathe. Use your Lamaze skills," he spoke and I wanted to rip his throat out.

"Fuck breathing! It doesn't work! The only thing that will stop this is when I push this kid out."

Carter's eyes widened as he stared at me. My insides felt as if they were being shredded. Dr. Perry walked in and examined me.

"You're dilated to nine, Zoey. One more centimeter and you can start pushing."

"Dr. Perry, please do a C-section. Let's just end this now."

He gave me a sympathetic smile.

"You're going to do just fine."

Carter continued to wipe my forehead with a cool cloth as I continued to scream in pain. I was exhausted and the hard part hadn't even come yet. I was more than ready to have this baby.

"Okay, Zoey, it's time to push," Dr. Perry spoke.

Hannah Avery Grayson came into the world at six pounds seven ounces. She came out with a healthy set of lungs.

"Oh my God, Zoey, look at our baby," Carter spoke with tears in his eyes. "She's perfect."

After she was cleaned up, Jessie wrapped her in a blanket and placed her in my arms. Tears started streaming down my face as I stared at her.

"She has your nose." I smiled at Carter.

"She has your beautiful mouth." He smiled back as he softly kissed her tiny head.

I handed her to Carter and he sat down in the chair next to my bed. As much as I already loved him, seeing him holding our baby raised that love to a whole other level. The struggles we went through at the beginning was worth it for everything we had now. My life was perfect in every way possible. He was perfect in every way possible. Everything for us had been planned since we were children and I couldn't wait to see what our future held.

****

Carter

Holding Hannah in my arms for the first time was unlike anything I'd ever experienced. She was so tiny and the most perfect gift from God. After Zoey had fallen asleep, I put

Hannah in the hospital crib next to her bed and went down to the chapel, where I took a seat in the very front and prayed. I knew in my heart that a thank you was in order.

"I know in the past I haven't been a very good person, and in some way, I don't feel like I deserve to have the two most beautiful girls in my life. I just wanted to thank you. Thank you for sending Zoey to me and thank you for the beautiful gift of my daughter. I'm a changed man because of her and I'll become an even better man for my daughter. I promise to take care of them and protect them for the rest of my life. I guess all I'm trying to say is thanks for giving me another chance at this life. You can count on me and I promise not to let you down."

My name is Carter Grayson and that was the story of how one special woman dragged me from the depths of hell and showed me how to live again. A woman who gave me two of the greatest gifts of life, something I never thought I could experience ever again: love and a family.

"Nobody can go back and start a new beginning, but anyone can start today and make a new ending." ~ Maria Robinson

Books by Sandi Lynn

If you haven't already done so, please check out my other books. Escape from reality and into the world of romance. I'll take you on a journey of love, pain, heartache and happily ever afters.

Millionaires:
The Forever Series (Forever Black, Forever You, Forever Us, Being Julia, Collin, A Forever Christmas, A Forever Family)
Love, Lust & A Millionaire (Wyatt Brothers, Book 1)
Love, Lust & Liam (Wyatt Brothers, Book 2)
Lie Next To Me (A Millionaire's Love, Book 1)
When I Lie with You (A Millionaire's Love, Book 2)
Then You Happened (Happened Series, Book 1)
Then We Happened (Happened Series, Book 2)
His Proposed Deal
A Love Called Simon
The Seduction of Alex Parker
Something About Lorelei
One Night In London
The Exception
Corporate A$$
A Beautiful Sight
The Negotiation
Defense
Playing The Millionaire
#Delete

Second Chance Love:
Remembering You

She Writes Love
Love In Between (Love Series, Book 1)
The Upside of Love (Love Series, Book 2)

Sports:
Lightning

About the Author

Sandi Lynn is a *New York Times*, *USA Today* and *Wall Street Journal* bestselling author who spends all her days writing. She published her first novel, Forever Black, in February 2013 and hasn't stopped writing since. Her addictions are shopping, going to the gym, romance novels, coffee, chocolate, margaritas, and giving readers an escape to another world.

Be a part of my tribe!

Facebook: www.facebook.com/Sandi.Lynn.Author

Twitter: www.twitter.com/SandilynnWriter

Website: www.authorsandilynn.com

Pinterest: www.pinterest.com/sandilynnWriter

Instagram: www.instagram.com/sandilynnauthor

Goodreads: http://bit.ly/2w6tN25

28720951R00147

Printed in Great Britain
by Amazon